# What's the Truth?

## Krystyna Stevenson

Order this book online at www.trafford.com
or email orders@trafford.com

Most Trafford titles are also available at major online book retailers.

Printed in the United States of America.

ISBN: 978-1-4669-7392-3 (sc)
ISBN: 978-1-4669-7391-6 (e)


*Trafford rev. 12/19/2012*

 www.trafford.com

**North America & international**
toll-free: 1 888 232 4444 (USA & Canada)
phone: 250 383 6864 ♦ fax: 812 355 4082

# Contents

To all women starting a new life
in a foreign country

# Chapter 1

## *After The Party*

Catherine did not stir as Paul came into the bedroom. She had fallen asleep with the light on. Her book was on the floor, where it stood like a miniature ridged tent.

Paul knew he shouldn't have stayed so long at the party. The fact that he suspected Catherine of having someone else didn't seem to be strong enough justification.

He tiptoed to her dressing table and stopped there, swaying slightly, looking down at those objects that women use to enhance the natural mystery that so enthralls men. He heard a rustle of silk and glanced up at the mirror. She was moving, stretching herself. Her long, fair hair was spread over the peach-colored sheet. Her tanned arm reached across the bed toward his empty pillow. She sighed and then settled.

He looked at his watch again. He was almost hurt that she did not sit up and confront him, ask him where he had been until four o'clock. When he dropped the change that he'd had in his pocket on the glass top of her dressing table, it was with a louder clatter than was necessary, and he watched to see whether she would open her eyes. She lay, though, unmoving, and he studied her in the mirror.

It wasn't true that one beautiful woman was much like another. He felt no desire for Catherine, but he could feel the eyes of the dancer mocking him from every dark corner of the room.

He closed his eyes, and the image of that woman dancing on the table came to him vividly. Her slender, naked form and those eyes that seemed to single him out, teasing, flirting, brought a surge of sensation to his groin even now with all that whisky in him.

He breathed in. He still could smell her perfume; it had taken hold of him when she had come to him afterwards in a close-fitting black dress. "Why just to me?" he wondered. And he heard her voice and remembered the anger he had felt at her mocking laugh.

"A psychotherapist?" he repeated after her, his incredulity giving his voice an annoying squeak. "And you take your clothes off for men?"

"A little hobby of mine . . ."

What interested her, she said, was the way men looked at her while she danced. "Dancing is control," she said. "Men get confused; they are unable to separate beauty from lust, appreciation from desire."

Paul turned from the mirror and gazed at Catherine. He was angry at her or angry at the dancer; he was full of mixed emotions, and it hurt. He undressed quickly and left his clothes on the floor, as his mother had never let him do. Was he angry at his mother as well? He didn't know. Then he slipped into bed and moved close to Catherine. She turned over onto her side, her back to him, without opening her eyes. He fitted his body to hers and put his hands over her breasts. She straightened up and turned over onto her stomach. He felt it keenly as another rebuff, like the one he had gotten from those scornful eyes, and he moved away and lay on his back with his hands beneath his head.

He felt possessed and frightened by this anger. It wanted to do some damage. He hated it, but also he hated himself for not being strong enough at the party. How could he allow this strange woman to have gotten so deep under his skin?

"Salivating animals," the dancer had said, laughing. He and his friends. All those solicitors, cool operators with perfect control in everything, except . . .

He saw them once again, standing around the table, their hands stretching toward her, and her mocking eyes laughing at them, her honey-colored thighs, slim and smooth, the perfection of the breasts, the vulnerable shoulders. Who had brought her to the office party?

"What power women can have," she had said later, looking at him with those eyes in which he could read the confirmation of her power over him. But he can control himself. He is not like his friends. He wanted to make it clear to her.

Anger and desire boiled in him. He wanted to show her; he would have her begging, phoning him every day, throwing herself at him. He would show her the difference between control and salivation. He would find out who she was, and then she would see. A mental picture of her dancing arose, and he kept it there, savoring it.

Then he turned and shook Catherine. She opened her eyes and rolled onto her back. She tried to speak, but he stopped her with a deep and searching kiss.

# Natalie's Diary 1

## Tuesday, 9 October

My dear Diary, my only friend. You are only one I can talk to about it. It was horrible!

It was no different from those German nightclubs. Worse, if anything. I had to dance on the table, and they came in so close.

I hated myself and I hated them. When I did it then, in Germany, it was for money, for Tricia. But now she has everything she could dream of.

I'm not really sure that my motives were entirely mercenary in those days. Wasn't it just to show Robert that I can make money more quickly than Catherine did? Everything was for Robert in those days. And still is. Unfortunately.

At least I know my motives now. And I'm almost sure it did work on Paul. But if it hasn't, I'll never forgive myself; it was far too degrading, not only for me. If those men could see themselves; they degrade themselves far more than I do. Men think with their penises anyway—how convenient for us. Thank God that I at least haven't lost my ironic sense of humor yet. I hate myself for using their weaknesses, but it's over now and only the future counts. So to bed! Beauty sleep. Can I arouse him at ten in the morning in the crude light of his office? Well, we'll see. I have to show him that I'm not just a body.

Wish I knew when David is coming back. Hope he finds enough to entertain himself in New York for one more night. How awful; I've used him, and now I have to do the same to Paul. Maybe I'll even have to invite him back home. If I have to, I will. You know me, my Diary, I'm not like that—but The Plan must succeed!

# Chapter 2

## *In The Office*

P aul sat behind his huge mahogany desk. His mail lay in a pile in front of him. He reached forward and pushed a button, but his secretary was already at the door with his first cup of coffee. He needed that, strong and black, he had a slight headache and was longing for the end of the day.

"What time is the first appointment?" he asked.

"Five minutes ago," she told him. "Mrs. Brown is already here."

"Who's Mrs. Brown?"

"I don't know; she's a new client. She made an appointment a week ago."

"Was she referred?"

"No, she just walked in. She asked for an appointment for ten today. I told her, as I remember, that it was a little early, but she insisted. I didn't think you'd mind just this once. She was very insistent. Shall I open a window?"

Paul nodded, and she went over to the windows which overlooked the street. She looked so fresh and full of energy.

He really didn't feel like any of this today, and a vague nausea swept through him. He tasted the coffee and pulled a face. The opened letters and documents faced him like an unconquerable mountain. He lifted the top letter and glanced at it. The typed words swam before his eyes.

"God, Sue," he said. "Am I going to have a chance to get through this today?"

She gathered the dried leaves from around a potted plant.

"I've kept the eleven to twelve slot open," she said. "Then at twelve there is Mr. Harrison."

"Him again?" Paul sighed. "What's after lunch?"

"Only three small ones."

"All right then, send Mrs. Brown in."

Sue leaned over, reminded him that he had hardly touched his coffee and left. He pushed the mail aside, then tipped his chair back and placed his hands behind his head and waited for the day to pass. There was a knock on the door. It was Sue again, with the client behind her.

"Mrs. Brown," she said, and stepped back to let the client in.

It was she!

Paul started, almost destroying the balance of his chair. He felt it slipping beneath him and righted it quickly to prevent himself from falling backwards.

He knew that she had seen it, because there was a look in her eyes that left him in no doubt, although she affected not to notice. It was a special look for him, and no one else would have seen it. It annoyed him that he had been ruffled so easily.

She was all in red. ("Aggressive color," as his mother would say.) She took a seat without being asked and crossed her long, slim legs. Her composure was in direct contrast to his confusion. Her smile showed her knowledge of his desire. She waited, her hands folded demurely. It seemed that she was mocking him again.

"Good morning," he said. "What can I do for you?"

"You didn't expect to see me again so soon, did you?"

He pulled his notepad nearer to him. Perhaps if he avoided her eyes, she would begin to understand his determination not to be drawn into any of that.

"What brings you here?" he asked.

"I want a divorce."

He was determined to keep it on this level.

"Of course," he said. "On what grounds?"

"That's for you to tell me," she said. "You're supposed to be the solicitor. And a good one, I've heard."

Somehow he'd gotten the impression last night that she was French, but her accent was like Catherine's: Polish.

"Unreasonable behavior?" he suggested. He wrote the words in the middle of his pad and underlined them.

"Not really," she said. "I don't think he's unreasonable." She paused as though searching for the right words. "It's hard to describe."

"Unreasonable behavior is the only ground these days. Everything can be fitted into that phrase. But first things first; let me take your details, Mrs. Brown." He wrote the name at the top of the page. "First names?"

"Natalie Mary."

He took her address and telephone number without looking at her, concentrating on writing them down, as though determined to form each letter perfectly. He wondered how long he would be able to keep this pretense up. It had not been a chance encounter last night. She had known who he was and engineered the whole thing. He was at a severe disadvantage. Worst of all, he could not rid his mind of that image of her, naked, dancing. If he looked at her, she would see what he was thinking.

"I can't stand this English distance and coolness."

He looked up sharply. Did she mean him? But she was staring at the picture above his head, and she continued, wistfully:

"He's such a snob. And so boring."

"But has he done anything?"

"Not that anyone else would notice. If s just . . . well . . ." She was searching for the words. "I'm much closer in sharing thoughts, jokes, with a total stranger than with this cold accountant thinking only about numbers and money. He's not my kind of man at all." She caught his eyes and held them. It was an unending moment, and a deep thrill went through him. Then she looked away at the oak panelling and his heavy antique bookcases, at the photograph of his grandfather with Queen Victoria at one of her garden parties, at his graduation photograph from Cambridge, and then back at him.

He saw mockery in her eyes now. His room. Was he a snob as well? Why did this woman make him feel ashamed of what he was? He could smell her perfume, and he wished that she were far away from him. No, he didn't; she made him feel excited. He felt alive. If she only knew that less than six hours ago he was fantasizing, imagining her.

"Last night I assumed you were French, maybe because of your dancing." He was angry with himself for saying it. He had altered the fine balance of the interview, and she lost no time in taking advantage of that.

"Is that what you thought? That only French women can be sexy?"

He remembered their conversation at the party now. He remembered that they had talked about women controlling men. As though reading his thoughts she smiled.

"What would you say if I told you that I did that just to provoke you?" she said.

"Do what?" he asked. She was mocking him again and becoming bolder. He looked down at the pad and very quickly at the picture of his mother in the right drawer. He would do with some help from her now.

"And so," he said, "you'll have to give me details of his behavior. And I need his name and the name of his solicitors. But why should you do that?" he couldn't help saying.

"What? Do what?"

"Well, you know. You said it. Why should you want to go out of your way to provoke me?"

She shrugged.

"Men do the same kind of things, don't they? If they find a woman attractive they go out of their way to well, to do something about it. Don't they?"

She was an extraordinary woman, even more interesting than he had thought.

"But you've never even seen me before."

"Ah, but I have," she said. "I know a lot more about you than you think."

It was getting out of hand, a million miles from the professional consultation that it was supposed to have been.

"What about lunch, then? To learn even more about me?"

"I'd love that." Her smile was radiant now; there was no hint of mockery.

# Natalie's Diary 2

## *Wednesday, 10 October*

My lovely Diary, my only friend! I'm rushing to tell you about the success! It was much easier than I thought in his office and later, at lunch. Paul is quite sweet, really, and I'm sorry for him. But what else can I do to get Robert? I'll play the role of a charming, sweet idiot tonight, again, to catch him. How I loathe such cold-hearted scheming. Taking advantage of someone's weaknesses, just like Catherine. Maybe I should be proud that I can do it so well, just like her. Ha, ha . . . obviously Robert would be impressed; it's the only way to impress him. Be tougher, quicker, more devious, as he was when he made me go back to Poland with three-week-old Tricia to avoid paying alimony. Will he believe that I've forgiven him for that?

But will I forgive myself for carrying out that plan? Especially if it didn't succeed?

# Chapter 3

## *At Natalie's*

B ecause Paul didn't know how to suggest moving into the bedroom, they were still sitting on the chaise longue in her elegant sitting room.

The minute he had arrived, Natalie told him that her husband was away on business and that her daughter was sleeping at a friend's house. Also, she had handed him a glass of champagne, so it was obvious that she was well prepared for the evening. Yet they still remained sitting on that Louis XIV chaise longue.

By now he had already stopped counting how much he had drunk. The only thing he knew was that she was beautiful and that he wanted her.

". . . the men in those nightclubs in Germany?" she continued, laughing somehow bitterly. "They were all the same but each with his own reason for being there. I could do a whole study on them."

Paul wasn't listening to her. Her face was close to his. He could smell her perfume and feel the heat of her body. She took a sip of champagne and moved even closer to him. Her leg touched his, and it was like an electric shock. She crossed her legs, and he caught a glimpse of naked flesh above the line of a stocking. She pulled her narrow red silk skirt down, and yet that was even more provocative. He wanted to touch her, but he did not know how to begin. He hoped that she wasn't sensing his agitation, and he tried to show that he was listening to what she was saying.

"Some of them actually told me that their wives sent them to clubs because they performed better in bed afterwards. After watching me dance."

Paul felt himself turning red as he remembered what he did to Catherine when he came back home last night.

"I hated those clubs and I hated my dancing."

"You looked as though you were enjoying yourself last night," he pointed out, teasing gently. "All those men."

"Men!" she spat. "More like animals!" she rasped but immediately softened. "I only did it to lure you here tonight."

She put her hand on the back of his neck, and he was filled with confusion.

"Would you have invited me for lunch if I'd just breezed into your office," she asked sweetly, "and if you hadn't seen me dance?"

"No," he said. "I never mix business with pleasure, and in any case I'm married."

"I know," she said. "I know a lot about you."

"Like what?"

"Like you are on the verge of divorce."

"Oh? How do you know all this?"

"I know lots of things." She smiled mysteriously.

It didn't bother him. Nothing did. He was aware only of her hand on his neck, caressing, and her perfume.

"What do you want from me?" he began. "I . . ."

"Can't you just allow yourself to believe that I want to seduce you?" She pouted playfully. "Just because you're a very attractive man?"

"You're teasing me," said Paul, thinking that even if it was only teasing, he wanted her to continue it.

"Teasing?" she repeated. "What do you mean? I'm serious; you are very attractive man."

The fact that her grasp of English lapsed was an even bigger compliment than the content of the words; Paul had already noted that when she was excited, her English suffered.

He caught her looking toward the fireplace. There was the Persian rug in front of it. Paul felt himself going red again at the thought of lying with her on the rug instead of perching on the wretched chaise longue.

Also he felt a little intimidated; she was always calling the tune, and he knew that it was time he do something about it.

He filled their glasses yet again and asked, "What should we drink to?"

"To us," she said, and there was no teasing in her voice this time.

While they were clinking their glasses, Paul took her hand and stood up. Natalie followed without resistance. He led her to the hearth and kissed her in front of the flickering fire.

She clung to him, pushed herself against him, and returned his kiss with an intensity of passion that he had only known about from dime-store novels.

He sank down onto the Persian rug and placed the glass on the floor beside him. She followed again, kneeling next to him, and put her glass far away. He pulled her gently toward him. Again there was no resistance. She replaced his glass on the carpet, putting it next to hers, far away, and he knew that she was making the space for what they both anticipated.

"You're so tense," said Natalie. "Shall I give you a little massage?"

He didn't know what to say. He didn't want Natalie to get the impression that he had been waiting for her to make yet another move.

"Well?" she prompted.

"If you like," he whispered, giving up his vain idea of taking the initiative. So he just lay there with his eyes closed, hoping that he had read the situation correctly.

She knelt beside him and gently massaged his shoulders. It was wonderful. He kept his eyes closed.

"Oh," she said. "You have such strong shoulders. I've heard that you play squash."

He sighed. He wasn't listening to her words. He only felt her hands on him and longed for her to touch him more intimately. But she didn't. He moaned, "Ohhh, I love you, I love you."

"Do you?" she asked sweetly.

"Yes, I do." He was sure of it just now.

"I don't believe you," she whispered. "All you want is to have your wicked way with me." He knew she was teasing him again, but her mouth was close to his ear, and the words blew gently into it. Shivers went through him, and he felt a hardness strengthen in his groin.

"No," he said decisively. "I do love you. I would do anything for you."

"Would you?" she asked softly. "Can you prove that?" Her voice was like the gentle whisper of the sea.

"Anything," he said. "Just ask me." He realized that he was committing himself to the unknown. But he felt ready for it.

"Stay with me tonight." Natalie's voice was pure temptation.

Of course he would! It was just what he wanted. Such simple proof?

"Wild horses wouldn't drag me away tonight!" With a frankness and fearlessness alien to his solicitor's lifestyle, he stepped into the unknown. This decision filled him with a long-forgotten happiness and freedom that evoked the times he would rush out of the school gates, playing truant, with his scarf flying behind him and a fire in his eyes that had not burned so brightly since.

"Let's drink to it," said Natalie.

"Let's drink to it," he repeated automatically, thinking how to express to her everything he felt just now.

"I love you," he began. "I have loved you from the moment I first saw you dancing. I'm not the type of man who says these things lightly.

In fact," he realized while he was saying it, "I have never said them before."

It was true. He'd never said them, not even to Catherine, those words that meant commitment. But they had come easily to Catherine one drunken midsummer night in Cambridge, and the natural consequence for Paul was Mendelssohn's Wedding March on a freezing February morning, the thought of which still made him shiver.

He heard Natalie repeating again, "Let's drink to it."

So they clinked the glasses, and Paul knew that he was at the point of no return, that he'd committed himself to leaving his wife. But it was exactly what he wanted.

"This is a bit awkward," Natalie said, and she put their glasses on the floor again, far away from them. Paul knew that he should just wait patiently. She straddled his body and sat gently on him. Her narrow skirt rode up so that he could see the tops of her red stockings, her black suspenders each with a small red rosette, and even a glimpse of her black lace knickers. He couldn't believe his luck. Catherine never bothered to dress like that for him. Why did Natalie?

Natalie leaned down and kissed him. He closed his eyes. He felt her loosening his tie. Then she started unbuttoning his shirt and stroking his chest.

"You have a hairy chest," she said. "I like that."

Should he say anything now? He didn't even know if he would be able to get any words out of his throat.

She continued stroking him for a while and then stopped. He opened his eyes and saw that she was unbuttoning her blouse. He realized with a thrill that she was not wearing a bra. He closed his eyes again quickly, pretending that he was completely submissive. He knew what he wanted, but he would wait to see how much of the the running she would make.

She leaned forward again, and he felt the brush of her breasts against his chest. It was sheer heaven.

"So you think you love me?" she asked, her voice teasing again.

"I don't think. I know I love you," he said in a very definite tone.

"I don't believe you," she stated dismissively. "You just want to get me in bed. I've heard it before. It's just lust."

"No, no," Paul protested fiercely. "I love you so much, much more than I can say. I want to build our lives together. You are my dream woman, the woman I've been looking for all my life. I would do anything for you."

It sounded to him like the lyrics from several love songs mixed together, and Paul was surprised that he could speak with such passion.

But his outburst did not appear to affect Natalie. She lifted her glass from the floor and sipped the champagne very slowly, swaying easily on Paul, her breasts dancing sensually. Paul felt that he was falling under her control even more. He realized that he had always let women control him, first his mother, later Catherine, and now Natalie. But there was no return.

"I love you," he repeated again, gazing at her breasts and placing his hands on her hips. A longing overtook him stronger than he had ever experienced, but it was short lived. She deftly extricated herself from his grasp, got up and stood over him with her bare, flawless back reflected in the heavy Rococo mirror over the mantelpiece.

Paul again felt powerless and foolish, particularly after his declaration. Now he really didn't know what to do next. But she seemed to know. She went out to the kitchen and returned with a new bottle of Moet. Paul found himself thinking again how well prepared she was the for the evening, just like Catherine when she had planned something.

As if confirming his suspicions, Natalie said, as they were chinking the glasses, "But if you truly love me . . ." She stopped for a moment. It was an eternity for Paul. "If you truly love me, you can prove it now."

"In what other way can I prove it?" Paul spoke formally now, taking refuge in the style he felt at home in. He got up and faced her.

Her reply came as if it had been prepared and stored somewhere, waiting all evening for the right moment to present itself.

"You can prove it by phoning Catherine and telling her that your marriage is over and you want a divorce."

Paul couldn't believe it. For once his habitual solicitor's caution was swept aside as he took Natalie in his arms and lifted her high into the air as if she were a child.

"It's just what I wanted to hear," he cried out. "We were thinking exactly the same!"

"If s how it should be when two people love each other." Natalie's words came between his in a matching tone. She was so beautiful.

"I want to be with you for ever," he cried again. "I love you, I love you so much . . . where is the telephone? Let's get it over with?

She brought it to him. He dialed with Natalie hugging him, her breasts pushing into his back.

# Natalie's Diary 3

## Thursday, 11 October

I should have suspected it would finish like that, when I saw Paul's state of arousal early in the evening. Maybe it's better it turned out that way. At least I didn't have to sleep with him.

I don't really need to sleep with him at all now. He has already promised to do all what I want, and his promise is a good, old-fashioned English promise, not like Robert's. Pity I can't love him instead of Robert.

I only feel sorry for him; he is so naive, just as I was when I first came here. So naive, with my Slavic, romantic nature. It hasn't changed much if I'm still able to believe in romantic love, for ever.

The main thing is to get Robert to come here, to London. To come and see me in my wedding dress, the one I married him in. And now I'm marrying his best friend, as Catherine did. And it impressed him so much that she was able to cheat on him. On him! Being so clever!

So now he should be even more impressed with me, "up cheating" his Paul and his great Catherine.

How nasty this game is! But it's the only way to get to Robert.

In the meantime, I have to play Paul along just like Catherine did. And despise myself for doing it.

So to keep things moving I should invite Paul to Spain while I'm there with Tricia over half-term. Maybe I should provoke him a little more. Yes, but he will want to sleep with me there because it will be easier for him, far from London and his guilt.

He told me a lot about Catherine, but nothing I didn't know already from Robert. It all only made me feel sorry for Robert again as I was when I first met him, when he was so suspicious about women, especially Polish like Catherine. Married him only to get a British passport and left him for his best friend. If he hadn't met that bitch before, everything would be different!

It's true that I fell in love with London when I first came here and that Robert was just like a symbol of that city: strong, happy, aggressive. But I loved him more than that town! And I wanted to prove it.

If s not all lost yet!

# Chapter 4
## *The Mountains*

" Golden fields covered with flowers, white houses at the slopes of the mountains." All around, it was just like in the song Natalie was singing. Paul liked her voice and the translation she was making from Polish. It wasn't grammatically correct but funny and childlike, and he felt himself being in love with her and everything around her. It was very good to feel that way.

The road twisted and turned on its tortuous path towards the top of the hill. Every few miles they would reach another sleepy village, each with its collection of skinny brown children and cats and kittens playing in the dust and gravel of the street and with the women discussing affairs of state in front of distressed doors painted in Mediterranean blues and greens. At the sides of the road, cascades of grass and wild flowers swung wildly from side to side as the car swept by.

Paul felt so relaxed and safe in Natalie's open-top red Porsche, swinging to her lullaby, that he started daydreaming again. Screwing up his face, he thought of their first night, when he had phoned his wife and then, consumed with guilt or maybe because he had wanted Natalie too much, had had his orgasm well before anything might have happened.

"Are you asleep, Paul?" Her question came as a continuation of the song.

"No, no. I was remembering our first night. You were very considerate about my temporary loss of form."

"Don't worry, darling," she said sweetly. "There will be lots of first nights for us."

She put her hand on his knee and moved it upwards into his Bermuda shorts.

"I see you are nearly ready for our first night again," she said and smiled, throwing her hair back provocatively. Then she started her singing again.

"Don't worry, be happy . . ."

But Paul wasn't entirely happy with himself. He had seen Catherine "the morning after the night before" and, without knowing why, found himself saying that he had been drunk when he had phoned her and, in fact, that he still wanted to stay with her. So everything went back to normal and remained in that state until he decided to accept Natalie's invitation to join her on her holiday in Spain. Is it possible to love two women at the same time?

"Look! How well you can see Gibraltar from here." Natalie's voice brought him back to reality.

She had stopped the car at the side of the road. Only a low sandstone wall separated them from a sheer drop down to the river undercutting the edge of the cliff. They got out and walked along the side of the wall until its abrupt end, where one brave pine tree rooted itself to the cliff's edge. Natalie leaned against its trunk, looking like a Vogue model on location, and said dreamily, "It's so beautiful here, isn't it?"

"Yes, it is," Paul admitted quickly, nearly mechanically. He wanted to be closer to her, to put his arm around her and to look together into the distance, which, he had to agree, was truly magnificent, with the hills in autumnal red falling towards Gibraltar and the sea beyond all covered in the gentle light of the late afternoon sun.

"It's so peaceful here," said Natalie again, looking into oblivion.

"Why can't life be as peaceful?" It came out against his will.

"Do you want to talk about Catherine?" asked Natalie.

Paul stalled for a few seconds. He didn't want to spoil the atmosphere between them.

"Don't you think I should know something more about her? You never told me how you met her, for example. Jut tell me about her. It might also help you in some way," she added softly.

"O.K.," agreed Paul. "But the story doesn't do me much credit . . ."

Natalie leaned closer. Paul thought that she was showing too much concern, but it was a part of her job; he knew that.

"Catherine was the wife of my best friend, Robert." He started reluctantly. "My best friend, Robert, who hopefully will be our best man at the wedding. I'm still not sure if he will accept."

Paul didn't really feel like talking about Robert, but she was waiting. "Just make it short," he decided.

"We were all at Cambridge, reading law. I should have mentioned that Robert and I were always great rivals as well as friends and that Robert was always best in everything, so not many people liked him very much. And that's why when our affair became public . . . I did say, didn't I, that Catherine seduced me one midsummer night in a meadow by the Cam? So when our affair became public, people were congratulating me that I had managed to defeat Robert at something at last." Paul realized his voice was shaking, but he was now determined to finish the story. He had never talked about it before. "It was a Pyrrhic victory. I lost my friend of fifteen years for a woman I knew was toying with both of us. Robert was humiliated, and he never spoke to me again. The rest you know. I don't really want to talk about it just now. I don't think he will ever forgive me such a betrayal."

"Don't worry, he will, he will." Natalie's voice was full of encouragement. "When he learns that you are not with Catherine."

"No, no," interrupted Paul. "It's not about Catherine—women never mattered for him very much. It was his pride."

"I think you should get in touch with Robert as soon as possible." Paul thought she was talking as if to a client but he didn't mind that. He wouldn't mind anything to get Robert back. "It will help you to resolve your guilt," Natalie added, less formally this time and more to Paul himself. "It's awful to feel guilty. Just as I do, all the time." She pulled Paul towards her; her mouth sought his, and her warm little tongue darted around his. But it was only a moment.

"The road gets better now," she said. "Would you like to drive?" And, not waiting for his answer, she added, "We don't really need to go to Ronda, if you don't want. There is a beautiful, old, white village called Gaucin about five kilometers from here, with a small, romantic restaurant. A favorite place of Tricia's father. It belongs to his friend from public school."

"Do you really want to go there?" asked Paul, somewhat put out. "To the place where you went with him? You are still in love with him." It was intended as a question, but it came out more like a statement. He didn't know why and he felt peeved. He didn't want that, either.

Her protest was too quick, too hot. Unnatural.

"No, no! Of course not! I couldn't love someone who wouldn't pay a penny toward his own child, who sent me back to Poland with a three-week-old baby and who only thought about his comfort, smoking his hashish day and night . . ."

But suddenly her mood changed; her eyes, which had flashed so fiercely before, were now overflowed with tears.

"I don't know anything anymore," she sobbed. "You might be right. Some things you just don't forget. You see, he gave me the most beautiful moments of my life, those evenings when he would shower me with flowers, and we would read romantic poetry in front of a log fire and discuss the idea of one soul in two bodies . . . I'm sorry," she said sobbing. Paul handed her his handkerchief. "I shouldn't talk about it now. It must be the mountains, or maybe you, being so friendly and understanding . . ." And she sobbed again.

She was so different from Catherine now. She made him feel like a real man, strong and confident, the man his mother wanted him to be. He put his hands on Natalie's shaking shoulders, and he knew that he wanted to protect her against the perils of life.

"I'm not sure how to say it," he started. "But I want to tell you that you can depend on me, for anything."

When he heard these words, they frightened him. He had never made such a commitment before. He couldn't understand it, either, why she started crying even louder now. "Don't say that. Don't say that!" she sobbed. "I don't know what to do. I don't want to use you. I'm sorry for you, for me, for all of us. If you could only know . . ."

She stopped suddenly and calmed down as quickly as she had burst into tears before.

"Let's not talk about it. Shall we go?"

But he didn't want to go. He was quite content, holding her in his arms protectively.

"Why don't you kiss me?" she asked; her head tilted towards Paul, her usual coquettish smile back on her face, while two big tears still rolled down her high, Slavic cheekbones. Her small hands gripped his back, her crimson nails making further creases in the cotton sports shirt his mother had bought for him.

Paul responded instantly, promising to himself that he should always be the one who would make the first move in future. But her kiss surprised him; it was as tumultuous as the emotions she had shown while describing "the best moments of her life," so he wasn't sure if she were really kissing him or the man she called "Tricia's father." "Why does she call him 'Tricia's father/ anyway, and not by his real name, whatever it is?" he wondered. But soon he forgot everything, lost in the passion of that kiss.

They walked back hand in hand to the hot car. Natalie handed him the keys, and they drove away, still ascending the mountains . . .

In a few minutes, they found themselves surrounded by tiny, white, typical Spanish houses. Their red terracotta tiled roofs appeared in various unexpected places, above or below eye level, because the village was built on the slopes of the mountains. Narrow, cobbled streets wound at all angles from the main road.

Natalie asked him to park the car at a small fork in the road, where there was just enough space for three or four cars and a similar number of tables. Two feeble saplings would have afforded some shade to diners, but there was nobody there, only an all-pervasive heat and dust. Natalie's hand was also very hot when he touched it as she was getting out of the car. Revealing brown thighs, she shook her loose, linen skirt in the sun, like a village woman would shake her sheets out of the window. Paul had to turn away and concentrate on the architectural details of the restaurant, La Casita, to prevent exploding from this sudden additional heat.

"You are right again," said Natalie, with unexpected sadness in her voice. "We shouldn't have come here, where I went with him."

Paul felt that she wanted to talk about that man. "Not again," he thought. But he knew that he wouldn't stop her, so he said, half jokingly, "shall I be your therapist now? I'm not as good at listening as you are, but if you think it would help . . ." He was getting hungry now, and he had already been thirsty for some time; he would rather have walked into the restaurant right away. But, in reaction to his words, she sat on the low stone wall in front of the restaurant, again looking like a model in designer clothes, and started talking to him in a slow, monotonous voice, like someone hypnotized.

"Mountains always have this effect on me. They remind me of the dramatic moments in my life. It must be their immensity; they are like God or a Great Judge to whom we have to account sooner or later. They smother me; I feel like I'm in a situation without a way out." She shivered, as if from the cold, in that hot weather. Paul never thought that memories could have such a strong influence on anyone. Or could she be talking about her situation now? "Unless I could fly," she continued, "as I did; going back to Poland with three-week-old Tricia, thanking God that her father let her fly with me, when in fact it was exactly what he wanted, so he wouldn't have to pay his alimony. How silly and naive I was, and how frightened of him . . ."

Paul put his arm around her shaking shoulders, and she looked at him with expressionless eyes lost in memories. Then she shuddered and clung to him, and in a second tears sprung back into her eyes, like when they had been looking at Gibraltar in the distance. And she said, coming back to reality, "I'm still unable to talk about it—I shouldn't even start—I'm sorry," she smiled warmly, looking genuinely apologetic. "Let's go in now." She got up. "I don't want you to starve here in Spain. You are my guest, after all." And she smiled again in her usual manner. "You can have a nice, big dinner," she said as his mother would. "We can even get drunk and stay here overnight, if you want. There are some rooms upstairs."

Paul thought the answer was obvious, so he just embraced her slim waist as they walked into the restaurant. He couldn't say anything; his throat was so dry and tight.

Inside was surprisingly cool and spacious. There was a fireplace that would be used in the evening, flowers and candles were on the tables, and several romantic-looking couples were already there. Natalie picked the table by the window with the magnificent view of the mountains, and soon Paul was at last able to relax, looking at the setting sun through the darkness of the claret. But they were not destined to be left alone.

"Do you see that lady making a grand entrance?" asked Natalie. "It's Diana."

Paul glanced over and saw a strongly tanned, middle-aged woman, undoubtedly English, in a loose, white, cotton dress, smiling and waving towards them. Her thick blonde hair was tied in a heavy knot, and Paul couldn't help but notice her large breasts and childbearing hips. Although she was not a classical beauty, she could pass as a symbol of femininity and warmth. All of this went through Paul's mind as he offered his chair with the view of the mountains while listening to the pleasant voices and laughter of the two women.

"It's lovely to see you again," they both said at the same time and laughed.

"Is this your new husband?" They laughed again.

"Not yet. Not yet."

"You were contemplating divorce when I saw you last year. Everything changes so quickly in your life that I might not be far from the truth." The woman looked at Paul again, and he read a compliment in her eyes. "And you seem so suited," she added.

"I'm glad you think that, Diana," Natalie smiled, putting her hand on Paul's shoulder. "I value Diana's opinion very highly." And she explained to Paul, "Diana is my best friend here, in Spain. Even though we don't keep in touch when I'm in London."

"I go to England less and less now," Diana said without laughing this time. "In fact, I haven't been there for the last two years. My home is here in Spain now." She directed this to Paul as an explanation. "I feel out of place in London, Spiritually, I belong here."

"Don't look so surprised, Paul," Natalie exclaimed with laughter. "I reacted the same when Diana told me about it the first time, she is so English. She was even more English then." And, turning to Diana, "You still look English," she added reassuringly, "even with your tan, peasant dress and slightly more Mediterranean figure than last time. But your posh accent is not so pronounced as before."

"That's what I wanted," stated Diana. "I feel more in touch with my real self now than ever before. What about you, Natalie?" she asked with a smile again, "Have you found your place on earth yet and your real self? Or do you still think that it has to be connected with the man you love?"

And she looked at Paul with a question mark in her eyes.

"We are getting married." Natalie's answer was quick and very matter of fact, so different from Diana's half-joking tone. "Paul is acting for me in my divorce."

"Another solicitor?" exclaimed Diana.

"Don't worry." Natalie was smiling now. 'They're not all as devious as Tricia's father. Paul certainly isn't."

By this time they had already been moved to another larger table, still by the window, with a "reserved" sign on it. Everything was going so fast that Paul felt like an actor in a film, the script of which he hadn't yet had the chance to look at.

And now the waiter was coming again, this time with a bottle of champagne that Paul knew nobody had ordered. In fact, he hadn't had time to order anything yet except some water and the bottle of wine, which by now was still three-quarters full. His menu constantly remained in his hand, and he was contemplating admitting that he was a vegetarian in the presence of these two sensual women, who gave the impression of being driven by basic instincts and the law of the jungle.

"It's on the house," announced the waiter grandly, uncorking the champagne. "Our patron told us that any time the Lady Natalie comes here, a Magnum of Moet must be brought to the table."

"Why is that?" they all asked nearly simultaneously. The women looked equally as puzzled as Paul.

"I only know that a friend of the patron pays for it," he said.

"Go on, Pedro," Diana insisted. "Who is that friend? Tell us."

"I can't say. I can't say!" cried the waiter.

"You must guess who it is," said Diana to Natalie. "Isn't it a nice gesture?" she added. "He must still love you."

"So what?" It sounded nearly rude. "If we can't live together—It's Tricia's father," she clarified for Paul. It wasn't needed; Paul had sensed that as soon as he saw the champagne.

As the champagne was frothing in the glasses, the waiter indicated that "the patron" was waving to them. Paul looked in that direction and saw the short, fat figure in the chef's hat leaning toward them from the kitchen door. The man was far away; the light was coming from the kitchen, and still there was only candlelight in the restaurant even though it was getting dark, already after sunset. Still, Paul could bet that he had seen that figure somewhere before, somewhere long ago. It was in England.

Natalie waved back to the man as if she knew him well. The patron bounded back, touching his hat in a military manner. Both women laughed. Paul was sure now that it was something official connected with that man in his past. It wasn't Cambridge, but there still was some air of authority around. Paul couldn't trace his elusive memories just now, because Diana was just proposing the toast for Natalie's and his happiness.

They raised their glasses, and Paul sipped his champagne, looking at Natalie. For a moment he saw her in her London flat again, with a glass of champagne in her hands, standing over him.

"Come on, Paul!" said Diana. "Why aren't you drinking?"

"I don't like to drink 'Tricia's father's champagne." He surprised himself with his frank answer. He nearly added that he didn't want to hear anything anymore about Tricia's father. Doesn't he have any name? Or is she still so in love with him that she can't even pronounce his name? Shouldn't he ask Diana? There is something of his mother in her; her opulent figure, or her warmth. That's probably why he couldn't lie to her.

His honest answer seemed to surprise all of them, and it might even have alarmed Natalie, because she suddenly started rubbing his shoulder as if she were trying to reassure him that Tricia's father didn't matter anymore.

And she said quickly, with a voice full of consideration; "Don't worry, Paul; Diana can finish his bottle. Can't you Di?" She smiled apologetically, then she looked back at Paul. "We will order another bottle for us or, better yet, a bottle each—for the start!" she added challengingly, in her coquettish tone again. "I want to have a champagne night with you. I want to swim in champagne with you tonight! Now, just let's dance! You can excuse us, Diana, please. I've never danced with Paul yet."

Only then did Paul realize that the band had already been playing for some time. Two couples were heading for the small dance floor. It was a tango. "La Paloma." He knew that Natalie liked it. She had played it at least twice in her London flat that evening.

She was already up, tugging his sleeve. Suddenly the only thing he wanted was to feel her soft, warm body in his arms again.

"Why don't you order something to eat first," asked Diana.

"You order something for us, Di. Just anything, please. Anything whatever for me," she added, pulling Paul towards the floor. "What about you, Paul?" she asked.

"Something light for me, Diana, please—preferably fish," he shouted from halfway across the room.

Natalie was already moving provocatively to the music. Her arms stretched upwards. Paul put his palms on her waist. She turned towards him, and he felt her breasts on his chest. He closed his eyes, and he visualized her naked breasts, swaying in front of him in her London flat.

He felt as if he were being watched. It was that man again, the patron, looking at them through the kitchen hatch. But he wasn't the patron before . . .

Paul was sure that he could recognize him now. "It was long ago, it was at school—at school with Robert—if s that prefect! He was the one we pushed into the mud on his last day at Eton, because he had persistently beaten up Robert while he was his fag! But it couldn't be he! The world isn't that small. If it is, I might equally well know Tricia's father. My God! Maybe that's why she never uses his name!" Paul's mind raced wildly.

The music had stopped between songs, but Natalie was still swaying, clinging gently to him. She whispered in his ear that she wanted to be with him "really close" now. In response, he kissed her ear, her hair, her neck.

The music started again. It was something slow and smooth. He didn't really listen; he moved with her, still kissing her neck. He felt drunk, and he felt angry. Was it with Tricia's father or with Natalie; still thinking about him? One clear thought persisted in his mind: he would never be able to replace Tricia's father. It made him feel sad, but it didn't stop his imagining her making "tremendous love or tremendous hate," as she described it to him once, to that man. To some man who wasn't Paul.

"I desire you even more now, as a woman belonging to another man," he said lightly. He wanted it to sound like a passionate compliment, but it was tinged with a deeper sadness than he intended. "But this someone else is not your husband. Not the man you getting a divorce from."

"I know that, I know that, Paul. I'm sorry," she interrupted. "I know, I shouldn't talk so much about my past. I'm trying to be happy with you, Paul."

"Trying? Freudian slip," he said sadly. "We don't need to try if we are truly happy. I doubt if you can ever be happy with me."

"Of course I can," she said quickly. "I know I can. I believe I can," she insisted, with that half-joking childish determination in her voice that he had always liked so much about her.

"Everything is about believing," she added religiously.

He pulled her closer, proving that he also wanted to believe her. But suddenly she said, in a very down-to-earth tone, "Let's eat something; I can see they have our dishes ready."

She was looking toward the kitchen. Paul saw the head of the patron just disappearing from the hatch. "It's definitely Frank. He has his chance to poison me now for what we did to him at Eton. Does he live here now, in Spain?" Paul thought.

Paul's pescado tasted superb. He drank his champagne and laughed with Natalie at Diana's story about her being a monk at the local monastery in her previous incarnation and her belief that it is why she felt so spiritually complete in Spain.

"I wonder if I will be making the same mistakes in my next incarnation as I've done now," pondered Natalie aloud.

"You mean you would let your next man smoke hashish?" asked Diana with a significant smile. "And dominate you, like . . ."

"Please, don't talk about it," interrupted Natalie rapidly. "Don't talk about it, please! Not now, when I'm on holiday with another man, the man I intend to spend the rest of my life with and who is the complete opposite of Tricia's father . . ."

Paul was suddenly quite sure that Natalie had interrupted Diana only to prevent her vocalizing that name, the name of Tricia's father.

"Let's drink to our holiday!" Natalie toasted vigorously. "To our time together! Go on, Paul!"

She became overexcited. Her eyes sparkled. She was so beautiful! But she was definitely drunk. He felt not far from it himself.

"Let's have some fun!" she cried out again. "Life is passing! It's too short anyway. We can't leave everything for our next incarnation. I might be a spider next time. You wouldn't like to kiss a spider, Paul, would you?"

She giggled like a little schoolgirl. Paul couldn't get used to her mood swings yet.

"Let's dance some more!" she shouted rushing towards the floor. He followed, as did some people from the next table, grabbing Diana.

The floor was full of dancers, and the patron was there, without his chef's hat this time.

"Hey, Paul!" he hailed, as if they had been best friends for ages.

"Hey, Frank!" Paul answered, while Natalie pulled him suddenly out of the circle and onto the stairs leading to the first floor bedrooms.

"Let's have fun!" she shouted towards Diana as a goodbye.

It was the last thing that Paul remembered.

# Natalie's Diary 4

## Sunday, 21 October, 11 a.m.

My Dear Diary,

I can't really write to you when I have David sleeping beside me, even though I know that he won't wake up after his night flight, long drive and stress that I wasn't at home. But I still can't concentrate with him around. Anyway, Tricia might come back from the beach anytime.

Thank God that at least she is happy, or seems to be. Just like her father, looking like someone who is on drugs most of the time. I wouldn't be able to take it if she started smoking hashish. She is at that age now. He told me that he started at fourteen. Maybe it's better then that she doesn't see him. It's strange, but she doesn't seem to bother very much—only around Christmas, when he sends his pathetically mean present: "Jointly for her birthday and Christmas," as he writes! Now, when he has so much money, in California! It's good therapy to write this diary. To keep me sane.

Paul surprised me with his lovemaking. Probably Paul surprised himself. And then Frank's knock and his message, that David phoned, looking for me. Why did he come to Spain? He must suspect something. He didn't receive our divorce papers yet. Maybe better that he is here now; we can have our open talk. He expected this from the day we got married, and it has made me feel even more guilty. He will understand. He knows I'll do anything for Robert.

Pity, I can't believe in reincarnation, like Diana does. In the next life, I wouldn't make these mistakes—I would just stay with Robert. I would let him do anything he wanted, even smoking his hashish. I would be a proper submissive wife. I must be going crazy! The next thing I was going to say was that I will even blame myself should he hit me again, as all battered wives do.

# Chapter 5

## *The Two Couples*

When Paul woke up, he realized that he was again being transported somewhere by car. This time it was in the back seat of an uncomfortable little Fiat or Mini. He'd been lying there, in the heat and sweat, and felt dizzy as soon as he tried to lift his head. There was full sunlight again, like yesterday, but the driver wasn't Natalie! It was his wife?!

"Catherine?" he asked, shocked, unsure of his vision.

"Oh, good! Baby's waking up?" It was his wife's voice and the usual sarcastic tone she used when she wasn't satisfied with him.

"What am I doing here with you? Stop the car! I'm going back!" And he visualized Natalie: How serene she had looked in that hotel room in a plain white nightdress that contrasted so dramatically with her black gypsy hair and bronzed skin as she lay on the old-fashioned brass double bed waiting for him. Her face so perfect, almost childlike, and so relaxed. Where is she? Where is Natalie?

"Where do you want to go back to?" Catherine laughed ironically. "You obviously haven't woken up properly yet." And she laughed again. "The hotel is already paid for. You checked out this morning."

Yes, it was true! He was now wide awake and completely sober. They were going to the airport! His weekend had finished. His weekend with Natalie! Where was she now? . . .

". . . Of course you wouldn't know, would you? . . ."

His wife was still saying something. Paul started to listen.

"You were still unconscious when I arrived. Apparently you were found at the bottom of the hotel stairs early this morning. You, of all people, falling down the stairs. You mother would be really proud of you."

Catherine was evidently enjoying herself.

"My pin-striped paramour was found on the bottom of the hotel stairs, in his silk pajamas that his mother gave him for our honeymoon, which, incidentally, you've never worn but instead saved for some whore . . ."

Paul started to protest but was cut short.

"I've been told that your tart left you in the middle of the night. So you probably were running after her downstairs when you woke up."

Catherine's voice was matter of fact, but it was obvious to Paul that she hated him.

"And you probably want to see her passionate letter left on the bedside table," she added coolly. "It will build up your little boy's ego."

She had it in front of her on the dashboard. And she read it out to him in the same cold, controlled voice.

"My Dearest Paul, I'm sorry, but my husband has arrived unexpectedly. You were wonderful. Will explain later." . . . Catherine stopped reading, looked at him and added: "I wonder when is she going to explain, and why, if it was a one night stand. Wasn't it, Paul?"

He knew it was what she wanted to believe. And he didn't know what to say.

She put the letter in the pocket of her blouse.

He knew it constituted crucial evidence against him. He didn't mind that. He only hoped that Natalie hadn't signed the note. He was nearly sure she hadn't; otherwise, Catherine would have commented on her Eastern European name.

"You should thank God that you're in one piece," said Catherine again, "and that I'm able to forgive you if not forget."

Paul didn't want her absolution. He remembered all her promises connected with a long succession of her ex-lovers. And he was thinking about Natalie again.

"It's too late," came out of his mouth as a continuation of his thoughts.

"Too late for what?" asked Catherine.

Suddenly he couldn't say anything. His head was spinning. He was going to be sick.

"Stop the car," he mumbled. "Stop the car . . ." he repeated weakly.

He was probably green in the face, because, as soon as Catherine looked at him, she sharply pulled the car to the side of the road.

Paul made the verge in time. As he was vomiting on the small yellow flowers, his mind started to relax. He made himself think about these flowers, and about flowers generally. He loved giving flowers to women. His mother—he didn't want to think about her now, but her voice was already in his head. "You should always tell the truth and never turn from the road you choose . . ." Why can't he be like her? The second violent retch overtook him now.

"Haven't you finished yet?" Catherine was calling him from the car.

When he clambered back, she tossed him a packet of paper handkerchiefs. Her mood seemed to have changed. She smiled, almost friendly, and said:

"We'll find you somewhere nice where you can have your cup of tea, and we'll all feel much better." It could equally have been his mother's voice. He didn't want to think. 'It's strange that, when you're married, sometimes you love and sometimes you hate your partner," she added in a philosophical tone. He only wanted his tea, to lie down and to stretch. And it was so hot.

After driving on for a while, Catherine broke the silence.

"Sorry about the tiny car. It was the only one I could get. It seems to have been a busy weekend for everybody. I was lucky to get any flight at all."

He didn't want her to talk. Her voice, or the engine, or the combination of both sounded to him like a dentist's drill.

"Why did you come here?" he snapped.

"I had to," she answered, still quite friendly. "The owner of the hotel telephoned and said that you had had an accident. Apparently he's an old school friend of yours . . ."

"You didn't tell my parents, did you?" interrupted Paul.

"No, I didn't," she said.

"That's something, I suppose," he sighed deeply, trying to relax again.

"This hotel owner," Catherine started again, "is he a friend of yours? I didn't realize that you kept in touch with anybody from school. You told me that Robert was your only school friend left."

"Yes, Robert was my only friend from Eton." When Paul was stating that fact, he realized how annoyed he felt . . . "What's that 'Spanish Inquisition' for?" he asked sharply. "Can't you see that that man is rather my enemy? A friend wouldn't bring my wife here and inform her about another woman. What did he tell you about her anyway?"

"Surprisingly little, for enemy," she answered. "Nothing, in fact. I found her note myself. He doesn't even know about it."

"He might have pretended," Paul started with his usual professional suspiciousness, but he gave up soon. "It doesn't matter now anyway. When can I have my tea?"

He realized that he sounded like a spoiled child. He didn't want that. He knew that Catherine waited for it. She liked him that way. She liked playing his mother for him. He knew that he didn't want that just now, but also he knew that he needed it all the same.

"We are only two minutes from Puerto Estapona," announced Catherine in his mother's tone. "There are several cafes and restaurants by the marina. You'll have your tea any time now."

He felt the car slowing down already. When it turned right and drove down the hill, Paul tried to sit up and look at the marina but immediately felt sick again. Thank God Natalie doesn't see me like this, he thought.

His eyes were stinging when he reopened them. Catherine was already looking for a place to park.

They were passing a line of restaurants with their tables standing outside on the pavement under umbrellas or canopies protecting them from the midday sun. It was already strong enough to make the customers, sitting there, look heavy and sluggishly static. It was this atmosphere of drowsiness that made Paul feel a little bit better. He imagined that they all must have had too much to drink the night before, so he didn't feel so alienated here. Perhaps his unshaved chin could pass for designer stubble.

Catherine eventually found a parking spot and parked the car, facing the harbor.

"The sun is awfully bright," she said, getting out. "You can have my glasses."

"Thanks," he accepted keenly. He wanted to look at the yachts. They always had a calming influence on him.

He got out and had a stretch. The yachts were beautiful, and so many of them. But he couldn't look for long because the sun really was "awfully bright" (as Catherine said), reflecting in the water and on the white sails.

He turned back to look at the restaurants again.

And it was when he saw her! Just opposite him, sitting at the first table of the nearest cafe—it was Natalie!

She looked stunning in a fuscia silk sundress that revealed so much. And the wind was playing with her skirt. She was talking in a serious manner, as if to her patient, to a man who was sitting with her.

Paul knew that she had noticed him also and seemed to hesitate, unsure of whether she should recognize him. She looked at Catherine locking the car. Paul couldn't guess why, but he knew that it was the sight of Catherine that made Natalie smile and wave to him invitingly.

"As usual, when I'm meeting you, I'm not in the best of form," he said to Natalie as casually as he could.

"That's how it should be with your therapist," she answered, also in a casual tone, introducing herself to Catherine. "I have really wanted to meet you for some time, Catherine," she added in a familiar tone. "It's always useful to meet my patients' spouses."

"I never knew my husband was having therapy!" exclaimed Catherine.

"I'm sorry. I shouldn't have said so. Anyway, that's how we know each other."

Paul was shocked that she could lie so smoothly.

"Please join us," she asked pointing at the table. And only then did she introduce the man sitting next to her: "This is my husband, David."

They all shook hands.

"The English are so continental when they are on the continent," observed Natalie, laughing.

"Your therapist isn't English, is she?" Catherine directed her question to Paul, but the way she stressed the word "therapist" was an open provocation, showing her suspicion about that woman unknown to her in her husband's life.

"Yes, I'm Polish," answered Natalie, before Paul had time to say anything. "And you are from Poland, I heard. Paul talked about you in one of the sessions."

"Only in one?" asked David.

"I'm sorry. I rather wouldn't talk about work now. We are all on holiday, I suppose?" she added lightly.

"Oh, yes, we are," exclaimed Paul and Catherine nearly simultaneously.

"Snap," said Natalie laughing again.

"Very unusual for one to have a wife and a therapist of the same origin," commented her husband.

Paul felt somehow uneasy in front of that quiet, hard working accountant, looking exactly the way Natalie had described him. And suddenly he felt a tremendous guilt, even stronger than in that summer in Cambridge when he also took another man's wife.

They were already seated, and a bottle of Mosel wine had arrived at the table. Paul couldn't understand how Natalie was able to carry on drinking after last night's champagne. In any case, he didn't want her to know how bad he felt after last night, so he decided to give up his tea, but Catherine had already ordered it for him.

"My husband drank too much last night, so he doesn't feel very well," she explained, as if he weren't there. "And we are heading for the airport now."

"How long did you stay here?" asked Natalie.

"Just a weekend," answered Paul and Catherine simultaneously again.

"That's not long," decided Natalie looking at Paul. Her eyes were asking: "Why is your wife here?" And he wanted to explain it to her so much, but he didn't know how to go about it just now.

"I'm also here only for a weekend," volunteered David. "But my wife and her daughter are spending the school half-term holiday here."

His voice was slow and peaceful, like all the surroundings. And Paul, lifting his cup of tea up, realized that they looked to the passers-by like two ideal English couples in an advert for a relaxing holiday in Spain. No extramarital affairs, no nerves, no lies. He would prefer it that way. Suddenly he felt very sad and very tired.

Natalie's husband, David (and Paul again had to pretend that today was the first time he had heard his name), was offering them some Spanish cigarettes. Paul declined, but Catherine, as though she wanted to surprise Paul's analyst with something she wouldn't know from their sessions, said:

"It would be better if you had some hashish. Early afternoon is the perfect time for smoking it . . ."

"That's true," agreed David. "We had such afternoons in Jamaica. You remember, Natalie?" he smiled to his wife. "We were smoking it in front of our swimming pool. It was a great time . . ."

"Oh yes," admitted Natalie, smiling back at him as if she saw that he was still waiting for that smile. "I wanted to find out what hashish is like," she added looking directly at Paul, with that impression in her eyes which she always had when talking about "Tricia's father."

But he saw her shaking it off.

"My ex-husband smoked hashish rather heavily," she stated in an emotionless tone.

"A lot of people smoke hashish," remarked Catherine lightly. "My ex-husband smoked as well." She looked pleased to have something in common with Paul's therapist.

"My best friend also smoked hashish quite heavily." Paul couldn't restrain himself.

"But don't forget that we are talking about the same person, your best friend and my ex-husband," interrupted Catherine, laughing at him.

"It's due to the alcohol," explained Paul, feeling like a complete idiot.

"It might even be the same person as Natalie's ex-husband," said David jokingly.

And it was then that it dawned on Paul that there might be more truth in this joke than David had expected whilst making it, especially since Natalie had become surprisingly talkative, as if she would like him to forget about it immediately:

"Rather impossible," she said quickly. "It would mean that there is only one man in the world who smokes hashish. But it is very popular now, isn't it?" She looked questioningly at Catherine, as if asking her to repeat the sentence she had produced earlier in the conversation.

"Oh, yes, yes. It's very popular now. Everywhere," Catherine confirmed almost instantly, evidently happy that she could serve as such an authority.

"When I went to Jamaica," Natalie carried on quickly, "I did a study investigating the effect of marijuana on violence in the family . . ."

"You didn't need to go so far to investigate that problem," Catherine interrupted so suddenly and so emphatically, as if she knew the problem first-hand.

They all looked at Paul quickly, and Natalie said to Catherine, smiling:

"You don't look like the battered wife to me. If anybody looks battered, it's Paul. I was just about to ask you, Paul, what has happened to your face?"

Paul didn't have time to say anything because Catherine hijacked his answer.

"You remember, I told you that Paul was drunk last night? And he fell down the hotel stairs. Just typical."

"That's what most of them say," smiled Natalie. "Battered wives, I mean. About themselves. When I see them for the first time."

"Do you treat many?" asked Paul, anxious to shift the spotlight away from himself.

"Dozens . . . as you already heard from Catherine, it's quite a common problem in England."

"I wonder," Catherine picked it up quickly, "if there haven't been any studies done which prove that women who have been in violent relationships have that violence imprinted in their memories for as long as they live?"

"Oh, yes! You also feel that way?" asked Natalie, but it was more like a statement of fact. "There wasn't a study done," she continued, "but there is enough anecdotal evidence supporting this claim; the battered wives' responses to any men in their lives are always conditioned by that violence. It means," she explained exclusively to the men, "that they are bound to view all their future men through fear-tinted glasses. Isn't it like that?" she asked, turning to Catherine.

"Yes, it is," replied Catherine. "I'm sorry; I have to excuse myself for a moment," she added quickly, already getting up.

"Shall I go with you?" suggested Natalie. "When you don't have a couch available," she explained with a kind of self-depreciating laughter, "a toilet is the second best place for women to talk. I always overhear a lot of personal stuff when I'm powdering my nose."

"No, no, thank you. I'll go alone," answered Catherine, rushing between the tables.

"Your wife seemed to be so interested in this topic, and suddenly she doesn't want to talk about it," observed David. "Not like mine, who likes dwelling on it just to get herself distressed, don't you, darling?" he put his hand protectively over Natalie's.

Paul didn't have time to answer or ponder about Natalie and David's relationship, because their attention was taken by the appearance of a young gypsy woman on the other side of the low whitewashed wall of the restaurant. She was bending over under the heavy load of colorful Moroccan rugs. She displayed them over the wall to Natalie. Two sickly looking children helped her to carry the rugs. She needed that help, thought Paul; she was noticeably pregnant.

Without negotiating, Natalie bought the first two rugs, taking some of David's reluctant money.

"Why did you buy them?" grumbled David after the transaction. "We've got almost identical ones from Marrakesh. And why didn't you haggle with the woman? It's not like you, darling. You taught me always to haggle when you buy things in Spain."

"There are times when you have to pay the price," she said philosophically, watching the woman shuffle awkwardly away to the next cafe, stooping under the weight of the remaining rugs.

One big tear went down Natalie's controlled, sphinx-like face. She picked it up with her finger-tip halfway down her cheek. Her voice was natural, caring warm, as Paul thought, she would use with her clients:

"Didn't you see the way her little girl looked at our leftovers, and didn't you see that the woman was pregnant? Those rugs may mean that she doesn't have to have an abortion. Might give her hope that she can afford to feed another child."

"You must enjoy getting yourself upset, darling," soothed David again. "Why don't you forget about the past?"

"You know I can't forget about the past," she repeated after him emphatically. "I just can't! I can't forgive myself that I was so stupid that I didn't even know about the existence of social security in England." And she added, as if explaining to Paul, "I just thought that I would die with my child of hunger and cold if he would stop supporting me. You know I can't forget about it," she turned to David again.

"Where is he now, your ex-husband?" asked Paul, to help her come back to reality, to the present, where, he knew, she felt comfortable—at least from a financial point of view.

"He lives in California now," replied Natalie. "In L.A.—the parcels for Tricia's birthday and Christmas are posted from L.A. We have no other communication."

"Doesn't Tricia ever ask about him?"

Yes, she does, but she is still at the age when children believe that mother knows best what's right for them. I think, I hope, anyway . . ."

When Natalie was saying this, Paul noticed Catherine maneuvering between tables. She waved urgently to him.

"We have to say goodbye," she announced, arriving at the table. She didn't ask for Paul's opinion. "I rang the airport; the next plane is in one and a half hours." And, she added in an apologetic tone, "I'm so sorry, but we really have to rush. It would be so nice to talk to you a bit longer, but you see how tired Paul is." It was his mother's voice. And it worked like hypnosis on him. He suddenly felt tired again, and the only thing he wanted now was his own soft bed.

# Natalie's Diary 5

## Sunday, 21 October, 12 p.m.

So that was Catherine, my role model, sarcastically speaking. I think Paul underestimated her. He might be right that she isn't a classical beauty, but her animal sensuality, her mannerisms, the flirtatious sparkling of her eyes, the way she seized the men's attention in the cafe today. Even those two gays at the next table followed her progress intensively as she slinked between the tables, leaving the heavy aroma in her wake . . .

I wanted to meet her for a long time. That "perfect woman"! How I hated listening about her perfection over and over again from that old witch, Robert's mother, and also from him. Such humiliation. I have to learn the way she ticks, as well as the lazy way she uses her body. It's so feminine! Anything to bewitch a male! Holding his hand a fraction of a second too long when he lights her cigarette, or his eyes—another fraction of a second.

I remember how much I had wanted to meet her long ago, at the time when I still lived with Robert. I wanted so much to learn all the features the ideal woman should have. I wanted so much to be his ideal woman. And nothing really changes.

I must emulate her. Be her paragon. If I'm not one already. And so ashamed of it, ruthless and strong, "getting anything she wanted," as the old witch used to say. Even the fact that she managed to "charm Paul to marry her" was admirable . . . Paul, the best friend of her husband.

I would like to see the old witch's face when Robert shows her the wedding invitation. And it will happen. It must happen. Now I managed to "charm Paul." How much better I must be than Catherine if Paul is leaving her for me. I hope it will be pointed out to Robert. It will be the first step to bewitch him.

How can I still want to bewitch him? The man who humiliated me, raped me, beat me and made me get rid of the child—how can I still believe in him? That's why I'm blaming Catherine for killing his trust, his ability to love . . .

I have to play that role. Playing again. Will I ever be able to be myself, to find myself again? Why do people always have to play to achieve something? Don't start your philosophizing. No time for analysis. Not now . . . just concentrate on following the plan . . .

# Chapter 6

## *The Wedding*

Already there, in Spain, Paul realized that to help Natalie was not a question of exchanging David for somebody else but to make it possible for her to get her second chance with Robert.

Already there, in Spain, he marked out this goal as his task. And that was why Natalie found it so easy to persuade him to marry her so soon after their divorces. Tomorrow's wedding was a part of his plan, and until now the plan was progressing satisfactorily.

Now Paul, a little apprehensive about its next step, was tapping his pen on the top of the desk in his office, looking with some envy at a surprisingly young Robert, who smiled confidently, tanned golden from the Californian sun, while he was taking his seat on the sofa, not, as he was invited, on the client's chair.

He had just finished his impressive speech, (Robert had always taken the top prizes for rhetoric at Cambridge), in which he thanked Paul for the distinction of the privilege of being invited to play "such an important role" as being best man at his friend's wedding.

Paul was just about to tell Robert who was going to be the bride at tomorrow's wedding, but he was postponing the joy of advantage over Robert, imagining the shock he was going to give Robert by casually throwing in the name "Natalie".

Never before had Paul felt so much in control over Robert, even when he had slept with Robert's wife. Looking at him now, Paul remembered again why Catherine had seemed to be so attractive for him in the first place; she was Robert's wife. He had wanted her but not so far as to marry. Now Paul couldn't stop to recall that on his wedding day, when standing next to Catherine and obediently repeating the words of the marriage vow, he was praying that Robert would suddenly appear and stop the masquerade, as he did in so many fancy parties at Cambridge, proposing sudden changes of roles and costumes.

And now he had Robert sitting in front of him, looking quite happy with the supporting role Paul proposed.

Paul nearly started to apologize that it was not a leading role, because Robert was known to play only leading roles in any gathering, but the temptation that he might tell Robert too soon his plan of developing this role into a leading role in the show prevented him from giving any details.

The script of the show, written by Paul and successfully directed until now, suggested that the "best man" would get a surprise the moment he saw the bride, who happened to be his own ex-wife. The plot, in Paul's script, was that the best man was going to steal the bride and take her to California to realize the dream of her life, which was to marry Robert again and live with him happily ever after.

This plot was not known to Robert, yet. This plot was to be born inside Robert's head as (as he would think) his, and only his, invention, as soon as Paul should decide upon it. "He had never had such a great advantage over Robert". This thought sounded repeatedly in his mind. He had never even been the play director in their student days, but now he had perfect control over Robert's action, even over Robert's thoughts.

Now he was the director of the final act of "Natalie-Robert's drama" and he never felt better and more in control in the whole of his life.

His only regret was that his mother could not see him; so much in command over people. Over their destiny, he could even say Paul knew that the only thing his mother would ask him would be why he was giving Natalie up if he loved her so much. Would his mother understand that he regarded enabling Natalie to have her second chance with Robert as a necessity to the future happiness of them all? Would his mother understand that he preferred not to have Natalie at all than to have her still dreaming about Robert. Yes, she might in fact understand him, he thought now, looking at the watch on Robert's wrist still on Californian time. Yes, she might understand, because she used to tell him many times when he was small the story of her first love whom she had never married. "So you are saying that your writing paid for the house in Beverly Hills?" Paul asked, just to clarify.

"Oh yes. Easily. And the snag is that writing is something I always liked doing. Remember our theatre at Cambridge?"

"Of course I remember. You are really lucky. Most of us do the things we used to like doing only as hobbies now, not as our profession."

"It depends how strong your will was in the first place and how much you were prepared to sacrifice to make in your profession."

"Are you suggesting that you sacrificed your wife and daughter here in England so that you could write your stories in California," asked Paul, trying to control the harshness of the judgement in his voice.

The answer which came taunted him or teased him as most of Robert's answers in the past, when Paul could never tell what Robert was really like or he prefered to take all this type of answers from Robert as a joke.

"Oh, no! Nobody is talking about sacrificing in this case, especially as I have never really like monotony and responsibility, both of which are unavoidable features of marriage."

Paul felt that it was too early to press this subject any further, so he smiled, taking Robert's answer as a joke again, as it was expected of him, and changed the topic.

"Which films did you work on? I have to admit that I have never heard your name throughout all these years." He took the opportunity to taunt Robert now, as Robert used to do all the time towards him in Cambridge, claiming that it goaded Paul to more productive work.

"You must admit," Robert looked at him with kind-hearted irony/'that you never used to read film credits and you hardly glanced at reviews. I don't expect you had changed?"

"I definitely would have noticed your name," retorted Paul, struggling not to let himself feel inferior to this man. Never again.

"Your fiancé," announced Sue on the phone. The announcement had come much too early. Before he had had a chance to make up his mind whether he should warn Robert who "the fiancé" was, she was already here.

He glanced at Robert, who looked as if he didn't need any warning or explanation. It was plain that he recognized Natalie straight away as soon as she entered the room and that he was probably prepared for their meeting one day because he acted as if she had come here only to see him, as if they were completely alone and as if she wasn't anybody's fiancé any longer.

Looking at her, Paul agreed that her red dress was most becoming and she looked even more provocative than usual. It took him back to their first meeting in his office, when her appearance, similar to now, caused his sudden arousal. But he quickly realized that now her sexy look was not aimed for him and suddenly he felt uneasy, uncomfortable in his own office, because he realized that he didn't exist for them at this moment. He was only surprised that he didn't like this feeling, since he had expected that it would finish this way in his script sooner or later anyway. Now he knew that he would prefer if it had come later, tomorrow at least, as he had planned.

Now he could only leave his office and let them carry on with the script on their own. Now he could only eavesdrop at the door, and he knew that it wouldn't give him the role of director influencing the actions of his characters.

"I'll make some tea," he said. "Sue is very busy this morning, and nobody else can make it the way I like. Do you want some as well?" He still kept his host's role. At least he tried.

"Oh, yes, please. Without sugar for me." Robert's voice was sober, as if he wouldn't be in his dreamland just now. His eyes were still on Natalie. Paul looked at her, but she didn't answer, her eyes drowned in Robert's. Paul didn't repeat his question. He knew how she liked her tea, and he remembered that the purpose of this exercise was to make her happy.

He left the door slightly ajar. He hated what he was doing, but he knew he was going to stay here, in this long corridor where nobody would come without being first announced on the phone.

"You don't take sugar nowadays?" he heard Natalie asking.

"I don't need sugar, having my sweetie next to me." It was the aggressive tone of a conqueror.

"Oh, don't be silly. Don't touch me," came Natalie's laughing voice.

"You shouldn't provoke me with your 'You don't take sugar?'" Robert laughed, imitating the way she had said it.

"It's my fault, is it? Again my fault?" She asked mockingly or coquettishly, Paul couldn't figure out which. He didn't even know what they were talking about. They seemed to have their own code of communication. In their minds they never separated.—He thought, sadly impressed by this short, infantile dialogue.

"I said, don't touch me." She was still laughing. "I'm going to marry Paul."

"Really? You are going to marry Paul?" His tone was teasing. "We will see about that. We will see."

They were a giggling couple of children. Paul as the creator of the drama being performed in his office, was pleased that his idea of "the stolen bride" seemed to be coming so easily and quickly to his actor's mind, but Paul, as himself, was surprised and sadly disappointed that it was happening as easily. But from having an idea to realizing it is quite a way, he thought, and he was curious how Robert would bridge the gap.

"What do you mean by "We'll see about it?" Natalie asked, and Paul knew that she did so to incite Robert's action. "There is nothing to see; I'm going to marry Paul tomorrow whether you like it or not. Why are you not supposed to like it anyway?" she asked provocatively.

"Don't play the sweet idiot with me. You know that I don't like sweet idiots and especially you playing one of them. We both know very well that you are not an idiot, so why are you going to marry that man?"

"I . . ." She started, but he interrupted, "Don't tell me that you love him. Don't give me any of that crap. We both know very well that you love me. And we both know that you belong only to me, and that sooner or later we should be together. Actually," he stopped for a while, "the sooner, the better in fact. Actually," he paused for a while again, "Why not now?" it was exclaimed as a discovery which had suddenly occurred to him. Paul was delighted with his actor following so precisely the script unknown to him.

"O.K. There is no need to shout," he heard Natalie's voice, suddenly cool and proper. "O.K. first take your hands off me, please. I heard what you said, O.K? But I haven't accepted you yet. Take your hands off me, please." she repeated in an even more matter of fact voice. Paul started to worry that Robert might change his mind, meeting this coolness in her. But she probably knew him better. "The only thing you think about is sex. As always, anyway."

"What am I supposed to think about when I'm with you?" He heard Robert's steamy voice.

"Yes, I know, I should take it as a compliment."

Robert seemed to ignore her mocking tone and continued unperturbed, ". . . when I see you with your little hairy pussy under your dress. Did you brush your wild little sister this morning?"

"Oh, stop it! Don't touch me!" He probably didn't stop, for Paul heard Natalie's giggling again, and he felt insulted through her. He wanted to go into the room now, but he managed to persuade himself that his desire to see the play continue was stronger.

"Did your little sister frown and get wet when you told her that she is going to see my little brother tonight? Look, do you want to feel how my little brother is getting harder as soon as we started to talk about their meeting?"

"Oh, just stop it, Robert, stop it, please. I'm not getting hot . . ."

"Aren't you, really? I'd better check."

"Oh, no, stop it, stop it, please."

"OK, OK, I'm not doing anything. At least you've forgotten about this wedding. You are not going to talk about this wedding any more, are you? Good!" She probably agreed, because his voice was getting tender again. "You know that if you need a fellow you can have me. Look, touch it. You can have me anytime. Do you want it now?" She probably protested, because his voice became impatiently aggressive. "Go on, here on the desk, go on! Oh, I would fuck you here on his desk now, oh I would."

"Just stop it, Robert, just stop it."

"You know I can't stop when you get me ready. I'll have you now! And you not going to marry this fellow. You know you don't need to marry him. You don't need to marry anybody. You don't need anybody now when you have your money."

"Remember, I'm not Catherine. I'm not for money."

"So why did you marry David?" His voice shook. "Why? To annoy me? You see, I know everything about you. I'm not here but I'm watching you. I'm watching you because you are my woman! You know damn well that you are. So why did you marry David? Are you my woman or not?"

She didn't say yes; she didn't say no, either, but she started to apologize. Paul was curious whether she was really so much under Robert's power or whether she just pretended to be to speed the intention in him to steal the bride.

"Remember, I didn't have any money when you left me."

"I didn't leave you. You were the one who walked out of the house. You were the one who took the child and went back to Poland. I have it on your declaration. You signed it. You wanted to live in Poland. He sounded as if he were defending himself, Robert, who was always right.

"We both knew how it was. We don't need to discuss it again." Her voice was worn. "If we love each other, that's all that counts."

It appeared to Paul that there was a questioning tone in her last sentence. If so, it was left unanswered. Robert said instead: "I never married again. I've had women, but I've never married again. You made me tired." It was not certain if always or just now. "I'm so tired. Let's sit down together as we used to."

"I love you when you're tired," she said softly. "It makes you so quiet. You see, it even rhymes." She sounded so happy.

"I would like to sit like that, quietly relaxed, forever." He also sounded happy. A different man. Was he acting, or was it a real Robert, unknown to Paul?

"Yes, I know, my Teddy." They even seem to have their nicknames, Paul thought with envy. "But you see, Teddy, we can't relax yet. The game isn't finished. Tricia will probably like our being together, but I'm not so sure about Paul. What are we going to tell him?"

"You can leave it to me." He now sounded more like Robert. He was getting back to action." I don't give a damn what Tricia and Paul think about it. It's our life! Tricia will have hers when she grows up, and I'm sure she won't ask us if we like it or not. But Paul?. Paul will like it.

I'll make him like it." Then he said, in a confidential, paranoiac manner, "He probably thought he could steal my second wife, as he did with my first one."

"He never knew that I was your wife." Natalie sounded truly surprised. "Don't forget that we were long divorced, and I was already married to David when I met Paul."

"Doesn't matter." Paul knew this tone. It sounded like a threat for him. He knew that Robert had already formed his opinion on the subject and nobody could prove him wrong. "Doesn't matter" he repeated stubbornly. "You used to be my wife, and Paul knows that he is not supposed to touch any of my women. He knows that."

"It rather looks like you are touching his woman," said Natalie.

"I'm rather his woman now. I was going to be married to him tomorrow."

"Don't talk about it! You know it annoys me. You probably like to annoy me, don't you? Let's forget it! What about leaving for California right now, instead of marrying this goddamn fellow? Great idea, isn't it? And if you're so desperate about marrying somebody, you can marry me!"

"Marry you? Oh, not again," she laughed, as if it was a good joke.

Paul started to worry that Robert might be put off by her reaction and withdraw his proposal, if it were a proposal anyway.

"Why 'not again'? Why not? It would be great fun?" Robert was evidently getting more and more excited about his plan. "You will like California. Americans are more in your style than English. You will like it there, I can promise you. I can show you how we make love down there." They both laughed.

"Oh, no, not now. You can show me later. Not in Paul's office. You'd better have his tea with him and tell him what we're going to do. I don't think I can face him just now."

Paul rushed downed the corridor to his secretary's office to avoid being caught eavesdropping.

When he returned to his office, Natalie had already gone. To his question of why she had had to leave in such a hurry that she had had no time even to say goodbye, Robert explained their present position in three dry, to the point sentences. They love each other, they are going to live in California, and the wedding is off. Just like reporting a case of somebody else. He showed no contrition or regret for what he'd done. Like Natalie, he also seemed to be in a hurry to get away from Paul. After all that I had done for both of them, thought Paul sadly. He poured tea for Robert, who went now on the attack.

"You didn't expect me to let you marry one of my women, did you?"

With Catherine it was a different matter. I was already bored with her, and she was becoming too expensive anyway, so I was even glad to pass her to you. But in Natalie's case you should have at least asked me if I'd already finished with her. As we always did with girls in Cambridge. You can see that I'm not really taking her from you. She is still mine."

Paul started to explain that he didn't know, but Robert carried on his monologue as if he hadn't heard him at all. "I know, you will look silly tomorrow, on your wedding day: an abandoned groom. But I looked the same, an abandoned husband, when you took Catherine from me."

"But you just told me, that you gave me Catherine voluntarily, so you shouldn't have a need to take revenge now, should you?"

"Voluntarily or not is one thing, but the other is how I looked in front of the world, an abandoned husband. Voluntarily or not is still an abandoned husband. But now we are settled. Everyone will say that swooping your bride away, in front of your nose, just a day before your wedding, is not bad revenge. Yes, not bad."

"You are not saying that you are doing it just for revenge, are you?"

"So what do you think for? Because of love?"

Paul was shocked.

"I don't believe you're such a cynic!"

"I don't see any cynicism in the fact that a man is taking a woman when it's convenient to him. She would always go with me. If I had asked her a day before her wedding with David, or a day after, or a day she met you, or a year from now on. When a woman really loves you you can have her whenever you feel like it and for as long as you feel like it."

"No, no, Robert, I don't believe you are such a bastard! You are not going to tell me that she is leaving her life, work, career here, in England, for you to leave her in a month or two?"

"It's her choice. A woman always has her choice."

"She has chosen you, because she thinks you love her."

"Women often think that they're loved because they want to be loved. We all always believe easily in something what we want to be true. Anyway, if s not difficult to convince a woman that you love her. As long as you do what she expects you to do, she will think that you really love her. Just remember to obey some rules. Like anywhere in life. Let her first through the door, kiss her when you come home. Anybody can do it. Anyway, it doesn't really matter if I love her or not. Her problem is that she can't accept me as I am! She couldn't in the past, anyway. She always wanted to change me. She even thought I should stop smoking. Hashish I mean. Funny women!" He laughed at the memory.

"When people love each other, they compromise," started Paul.

"OK, OK, It's as if I would hear her again. Is she paying you to be her solicitor? It looks as if you would like me to live with her. Maybe you two had everything arranged, as I had with Catherine to catch you? But even if so, I don't mind. The main thing is you will look silly tomorrow on your wedding day, and I'll manage somehow with Natalie. As I've managed until now. In bed she is first class, and this is the main thing! Tell me how did you manage with her in bed?"

"Your mother is on her way down the corridor." It was Sue's voice on the phone. It acted like a bucket of a cold water on Paul's head. It cooled his anger towards Robert, but it didn't provide him with the answer what to tell his mother regarding the wedding. He felt he couldn't tell her about cancelling it just now. It would be unfair to her. He would feel like taking revenge on her because somebody else had given him a shock. He couldn't pass it to her. Not just now.

"I'm going out with you; we have an important meeting," he said quickly to Robert.

"OK, coward," laughed Robert, in answer.

Paul didn't mind it. He preferred to be mocked than to face his mother. He didn't want to lie to her, and he knew that he would have to do it if she confronted him right now. If he started: "Robert's stolen Natalie from me," his mother would interrupt along the line, "Didn't

I tell you that you shouldn't invite him at all. Wasn't is obvious that he hasn't forgiven you for taking Catherine and that he was waiting for his opportunity to take revenge? So you put this opportunity right in his hands. "And she would go on and on how ambitious Robert had always been and that having known him for so long it was obvious that he was incapable of accepting defeat.

Paul would admit she was right because he was capable of accepting defeat. But he didn't want to talk like that with her. He wanted to tell her the whole truth. He felt he had to tell the whole truth to somebody, he had to talk about it, otherwise he might get crazy, knowing all his sacrifices were wasted. He wanted to sit at her knee as he used to do long ago, when he was a boy, and admit his mistake, his disappointment with his ideal, with his hero, Robert, his regret that he had loved him so much and for so long. He wanted to tell her, with his head on her knees, how much he loved Natalie and how much he worried about her future. He would like to admit that he was so much under her influence that he had agreed to prepare this arranged wedding only because he wanted to bring Robert to England and induce him to take Natalie away. He would like to tell her that he had agreed on this role of abandoned fiancé, the role he had to play now to the shame of his mother and all his family, because he wanted so much to make Natalie happy. But mainly he wanted to tell her how sorry he felt for Natalie just now because until now he believed that Robert still loved her.

He looked at Robert, playing the role of charmer, as he always did, in the presence of women. Right now he was kissing the hand of Paul's mother, greeting her in the European style, and symbolically paying homage towards women whom, as Paul knew, he despised.

Maybe I'm wrong, thought Paul. Maybe Robert is only showing off in front of me, telling me how much he despised women. Maybe he really loves Natalie. Maybe he will start to treat her as a husband should, when they will marry? It would mean I would lose her forever. OK, God. Just let her be happy, after all she's gone through.

# Natalie's Diary

## Saturday, 29 June

Why do I still let him treat me in this way? Like before. As if I wouldn't be anything else, only a sex object.

Is it because I'm not sure whether he can find anything interesting in other aspects of myself? And I so desperately want him to be interested in me? . . . Is it my inferiority complex talking again? A complex which I developed here in England where I'm always only a bloody foreigner regardless what I would do. Isn't it funny? Because the English have no interest in other countries and people, I developed an inferiority complex? And because of my inferiority I took as a compliment Robert's saying that I can arouse him like nobody else. As if arousing him was the primary goal of my life. But maybe it is. Unconsciously, even if I fight against admitting it. Maybe it should be, if I really love him. Maybe it's the role of a woman in love, regardless of country and class.

It was my role yesterday anyway. I was a submissive wife, a woman in love, a living example of anything I hold in contempt and fight against as a feminist. A subordinate wife, asking by her behavior to be ignored and humiliated because she regards herself as an object belonging to him or as something specially created to serve him.

It started again the moment I saw him. And I couldn't help it even though I'd promised myself never to behave in that manner again. But intuitively I felt that this was the way he wanted me to respond, the way he wanted me to be, otherwise he wouldn't want me. Otherwise he wouldn't ask me to go to California with him, and I wouldn't be on this plane just now.

I know, I'm trying to justify my behavior in front of my feminist half.

Bust also if s true that I was dreaming about this moment for years. To sit next to him on the plane to California. It was all I wanted! And I've succeeded! So I'm happy! I should be happy! We are happy together. Is he happy?! He must be happy! Just exhausted. That's why he is asleep. Everything will be OK. In California all husbands are better. So why are there so many divorces? It's simple: women are not so afraid of the stigma of being divorced and have more possibilities afterwards than we do here. Maybe it's why husbands are better. They are more afraid of divorce and the money they have to pay. All men are like little boys. They have to be kept under the threat of losing something. If not a wife who is loved, then the money at least. In Robert's case the only thing he doesn't want to lose is his hashish. His money as well, I suppose. It's strange that he asked me to go so quickly without taking any money. As if he'd stopped counting every penny he spent on me or the child. Maybe he feels guilty that he hadn't given me any money throughout all these years. Or maybe he has too much money in California. But he never would have too much. That's what Paul said, and he hoped it's the case. At the airport yesterday, he was more cynical toward Robert than ever before. Why? Last moment realization and jealousy? Even though all the time before he wanted me to go, wanted me to have my second chance with Robert, as we called it? My second chance with Robert. I'll really do everything for it. I'll not have myself to blame if it doesn't work.

How great it'll be to have the home I always wanted. Tricia not in boarding school, maybe another child when Paul visits us in a year's time. Hopefully with his new girlfriend, as he jokingly promised me at the airport. I owe him so much! I do believe that he really wants my happiness. If he would know how much I want him to be happy. All of us happy together like the big family, that I always dreamed about.

# Chapter 7

## *In California*

A nd he again felt the same responsibility towards this girl as he had at the moment when they landed five days ago at LAX (not as big as he expected), when she said, "I'm a little bit afraid to meet them, because Mummy is always somehow different when Daddy is around".

He had also already noticed this change in her. Natalie really seemed to be a different woman from the time he had last seen her nearly a year ago. Not that she had altered physically in any way, although she seemed younger, as if she wanted to look like those eternally smiling, on the make, colorful, self-confident, dangerous women whom Paul had had the opportunity to meet yesterday at Robert's party in his Beverly Hills residence.

But there was this permanent tension and fright, similar to that of a film director who is unsure if he has chosen the right actor for the main part in his film. Yes, this was the change: the constant doubt about what tomorrow would bring. And, in fact, there was nothing unusual about her worry if the main character were played by Robert.

However, until yesterday's party, Robert had played his role so well that Paul was forced to give up all his hidden expectations that Natalie might ever come back to him. Her life here, with Robert, seemed by English standard rather too good. As if taken straight out of a movie. Too sweet, too rich, too colorful and too happy. But this was probably the norm here—the more and bigger, the better, and if you have it, flaunt it. In fact, her life here looked even more happy than he had imagined from her regular monthly letters which indirectly warned him that he shouldn't accept the holiday invitation if he was going to be afraid of the pangs in his heart when he saw her radiant with another man. Even yesterday morning he was still considering an excuse to make his stay shorter: Robert masqueraded so well. Until yesterday's party when, maybe under the influence of a mixture of alcohol and hashish, or maybe because he was already bored with playing the role of the ideal husband, he quite casually started fondling the breasts of one of the script-girls.

Just now they were finishing breakfast in the bright sunny and spacious kitchen. It was proceeding as usual in its warm everyday family atmosphere, just as if everything had been forgiven and forgotten. And it was then that he suddenly felt this responsibility towards Tricia, at the moment when Natalie threw in her normal tone, almost as like between the lines of what she was just saying: "Look after my child, Paul". Only her eyes revealed the seriousness of this request, as she leant towards him across the table, just when the other two, Robert and Tricia, seemed to be absorbed in jokes and talk.

They were sitting on opposite sides of the long, bare, oak kitchen table, with Paul and Tricia facing the bright light from the huge window overlooking the garden. The reflection of the sun from the swimming pool flickered in Tricia's eyes whenever she looked at Paul. But that happened not often, because most of the time her eyes were fixed on Robert.

Paul liked these informal breakfasts. They reminded him of his parents' house when the maid had her day off. He noticed that Robert seemed to gain great pleasure from teasing Tricia and that the child's face, like always when listening to her father's stories, expressed fright at the same time as asking for more. "What are you laughing at so much?" asked Natalie, directing her question to her daughter.

"Daddy is telling me how Grandad put him into the cellar and that real rats were there . . ."

"Daddy already told you about it many times when you were smaller, and you know that I don't like when he tells you this story, so why again now?" It was still directed only to Tricia.

"Because this cellar which we have here is exactly the same as grandad's and there might be rats there as well," answered Robert in the tone of the mischievous child. "And do you know what rats can do when . . ." He turned towards Tricia again, but Natalie interrupted rapidly.

"We will talk about it another time." Tricia seemed to be disappointed but didn't raise any objection. "Now we should hurry to the beach," continued Natalie.

"But you can't go," protested Robert. "Have you forgotten, you have appointments with your hairdresser and your beautician?"

"I'm just thinking if not to cancel it," said Natalie meditatively. "We've forgotten to warn Paul," and she turned toward him with a note of apology in her voice, "that today we have another party. At Nicola's. You met her yesterday, remember?"

Yes, he remembered. Brash, dyed platinum, brash, garish dress.

"You really should go to the beautician," insisted Robert. "Parties night after night; it's too much at your age."

"It somehow doesn't affect you," answered Natalie.

"Because I smoke hashish." He seemed to have for everything his light, jovial answer. "I'm always telling you to do the same," he added, getting up from the table and not waiting for her to answer. He said, "I will show them Malibu. Maybe also the Getty museum, if we have time. In ten minutes at the car," he shouted to Paul and Tricia, as if it had already been decided that Natalie was not going with them. And he was already out of the kitchen and out of range of their voices if they wanted to protest.

Natalie was clearly angry.

"And he again frightens the child with the cellar. And what for? To give her stress? Just like when she was little and didn't want to eat. So he frightened her that he would lock her in the cellar. Once when I eavesdropped at the door," she remembered, "he was describing musty smelling, in colors without the light, life of the rat population down there. The child was choking herself with food and coughing because her throat was constricted from fright. Do you remember that, my sweet dumpling?" She still called Tricia "her dumpling" in the moments of family intimacy, even though this long-legged, very slim, thirteen year-old girl didn't look any more anything like a round, fat dumpling.

"I don't remember anything like that," protested Tricia looking somehow surprised that anything like that did happen.

"Isn't it strange?" said Natalie wistfully. "I have already noticed before that she never remembers anything negative about her father. Freud must be right with his family patterns."

"I remember something else about rats," interrupted Tricia impatiently, who probably wanted to prove to her mother that she did remember her childhood, with Mum and Dad being together. "I remember when Daddy told me that Grandad locked him up once in the cellar, for the whole night. And I was so angry with Grandad that I never let him carry me around the garden again."

"You see, you see?" Natalie turned towards Paul. "Didn't I say so?" There was fright in her voice when she came closer to Paul, and, looking deeply into his eyes, she repeated as at breakfast: "look after my child, Paul." And quickly she moved back towards Tricia and added gaily: "The cellar is not the right topic on such a beautiful day. You two have to relax now. Don't forget you are on holiday. Isn't it beautiful here?"

"Oh, yes, yes, it's so lovely here," shouted Tricia enthusiastically.

"You haven't seen Malibu beach yet, darling. Pity I can't go with you." Natalie looked as if she were wavering inside, but Tricia carelessly came into her sentence:

"We can go there tomorrow again. You can go tomorrow with us, can't you?"

Did she accept so obediently her father's authority, or does she herself prefer that her mother wouldn't go? went through Paul's mind.

"Yes, I suppose so," agreed Natalie. "Hurry up now. I can hear that Father has already got the car out. Make sure you will not stay too long in the sun." She acted as if she would be the mother of both of them. And, as Paul had the opportunity to notice before, she usually arranged that he and Tricia, it means "packet from England" (as they were already called here) were always together. No doubt she was avoiding being alone with him, as if she would be afraid that he would start to inquire about her life here with Robert. Because he couldn't see any other reason.

Paul enjoyed the Getty museum very much: French furniture; the desk in the style of Louis the Sun King, much smaller in fact than the one in Versailles, but it would be just the right size for his mother, he thought. He knew she would love to have even a nineteenth century reproduction of it. He caught himself again in the realization that, as he was getting older, he appreciated his mother's style and values more and more.

They had just finished with the interior of the museum and stopped for a while in the garden to admire the huge decorative pool; evaporating some humidity on the perspiring tourists, on the flowers, shrubs, and statues around.

In front of them were two rows of statues of young maidens, slender, proudly erect, their hands raised above their heads. One of the statues was missing, and Robert proposed that Tricia replace it for a photo, posing like the others.

Tricia was more than keen, her usual reaction to anything her father suggested. She immediately jumped gracefully onto the empty pedestal and lifted her arms in a pose resembling the statue opposite. Even her face changed as she adopted her neighbor's spiritual characteristics forged in stone.

Robert looked at her through the camera lens and didn't seem to be satisfied.

"Could you push your breasts out a little more?" He demanded. "You have really good breasts, so you shouldn't be ashamed of them. Look how these statues are showing off their breasts. It's necessary, as far as breasts are concerned," he went on in the tone of a connoisseur, "to make sure that you can see the nipples through the material. Wait a moment: I'll do it for you," he decided. "Jump down for a minute." And he took her hand, as she was getting ready to jump. Suddenly he pulled her towards him, pretending it happened by accident, and said laughing: "Oh, Tricia, how clumsily you jump. I thought my daughter would be a little more agile."

It wasn't true! She hadn't jumped clumsily! Paul had seen it. Should he say something? But Tricia didn't seem to be offended. She laughed gaily at the joke while still remaining close to her father in his arms.

"Now I can form your nipples to look just right for the photo? What are you frightened of? You see what one has to do for art?" he added explainingly toward Paul, and turned to Tricia again: "They need a little massage to make them stand up." And he laughed again, provoking Tricia's laughter, as he repeated: "You see how we have to sacrifice ourselves for art—but don't worry, you will have a super photo. I guarantee that."

Tricia protested initially; when he touched her breast for the first time, but later on she only laughed, as if she really regarded it as a good joke. Or maybe she chose this as a strategy, thought Paul, while she turned her back toward Japanese tourists who were just passing by. She must feel it is wrong, he thought again, and still he didn't know how he was supposed to react. In the end Robert is her father; he must know when a joke should stop. But, on another hand, it was Paul who was asked to look after Tricia. But surely not against her own father. Maybe I shouldn't be so sure about it? How should he react to this strange behavior? *Was* it strange behavior? Maybe it was quite normal behavior between fathers and daughters(?). He wasn't sure one way or another. He realized that he didn't really know any fathers with teenage daughters, or not so close anyway. So he started looking for comparisons in his own childhood. He was also quite close to his mother, probably not so close, he quickly corrected his memory, overwhelmed for a second by love and respect for his mother.

When they had finished with this photo, on which, and Paul knew something for sure at last, Tricia's breasts would undoubtedly look very sexy, Robert decided that he wished to have a series of photos with his "darling daughter". And this was when real father–daughter intimacy started. There were all kind of embraces and touches which were skillfully interlaced with jokes explaining their "necessity".

Tricia couldn't even sit peacefully on the marble bench, posing for the picture entitled by Robert "Relaxing Beauty," because even there Robert's hand found the spot, just before she sat down, with the information of the attentive father that "marble at this time of the year in California might be too hot." His hands seemed to be everywhere.

But the worst was that Paul was not entirely sure that Tricia's playful protests were 100 percent sincere. One thing he was quite certain of was that this adoration of her father pleased her tremendously. He suddenly remembered that it was Tricia who cut off Natalie's wavering at breakfast as to whether she should go with them to Malibu. Couldn't it be true that Tricia was jealous of the attention her father has given to Natalie? Yes, that's right! And Paul remembered how as a child he used to like going somewhere with his mother alone, to get her undivided attention–Is it due to the amount of drinks I've consumed that I'm enjoying this party more and more? thought Paul, as he joined the next group of Nicola's guests, standing with champagne glasses in their hands next to another drink trolley on the opposite side of the wooden dance floor, which had been skilfully placed in the center of the garden.

It must be due to the drink, because only an hour ago he still thought that there was far too much music and noise, far too much drink on the bars and the trolleys everywhere in the garden, and too much food on the barn tables on both sides of the dancing floor. But by now he was quite happy about everything here and quite keen to admit that this was exactly like an Italian Wine Festival should be.

Nicola was a second generation American, as Paul had been told when they were introduced, and her grandfather, a vineyard owner from Tuscany, always helped her to prepare her annual parties, which were so truly Italian that even the grandfather himself called them "an Italian Wine Festival in California."

Paul was also told that Nicola's parties were so greatly appreciated here that they were talked about long after, not only by the Italian community of L.A. and Santa Barbara but also by Americans of eight or ninth generations, who would fly in specially for the occasion from places as far as Philadelphia and New York.

As Paul started to feel more at ease with the Italians and all the surroundings, he began gradually to spend less and less time with the various groups of people, listening to their conversations, and found himself coming back more often to one particular drinks trolley, with whose bottles' architecture he had become most familiar.

On each of these approaches he heard distinctly his mother's voice, as if it had been wafted by the gentle gusts of wind from the nearby hills. The voice was warning him, "Never mix drinks, Paul." He was in a very conciliatory mood. He didn't mix them then, but also he didn't drink them neat, like Robert did, in the Polish style. If I'm drunk, I don't want to think what Robert is, he thought.

"Hi, Paul. I always see you at the bar. Which drink are you on?"

Natalie was standing next to him. Beautiful and relaxed, slender, looking taller in her long red dress, "Her favorite color," he mused, emphasizing the golden tan on her bare neck, shoulders and back. It could be touched while dancing. I have to dance with her.

"I don't know. I stopped counting them," he answered. "But I'm pouring a lot of water and not so much whisky. It's very hot here; even the hills don't help much." He said this as a half-question, looking for a topic to make her stay. She wasn't in a hurry.

"Nicola lives beautifully, doesn't she?" she stated. "And the view down there, oh, marvelous." He turned, and they looked together, arm in arm, on Universal Studios beneath their feet, the lights of L.A. in the distance and the large "Hollywood" sign over on the right, on the neighboring hill.

"Do you remember when we were looking down on Gibraltar in the distance on our day in Spain?" asked Paul, trying to get intimate with her. "It was as hot as it is now, and . . ." he looked at her and, seeing that, just as at that time in Spain, she was falling into a lethargy, he knew that he had to finish his sentence thus: "and you also had those vacant eyes."

She shook herself instantly: "Oh, yes, I remember. It always happens when I think of Robert."

"Do you often think about him?" asked Paul.

She took it as a statement, not a question. "I know, Paul. Too often." She said it pensively but almost immediately she changed her tone, as if coming back to reality, and wanted to reassure him that reality was good, gay, positive, and added: "You should know, how funny a relationship I have with Nicola. It's based on 'mutual contradiction' or 'contradicting each other/ it could be said. Come and listen to our discussion. People have great fun, when they see us together . . . She is such a snob. And she loves to pretend that she knows a lot more than she really does. About everything. For example, a wine. Come and tell her that she shouldn't keep her wine in the kitchen. It's far too hot there. I just told her that, but she knows better, of course. Since the rugs are designed for there, the wine should be kept there, she says, especially as it looks good. She does everything for looking good; real quality doesn't count. You can tell her that, can't you? Some bottles are leaking already, anyway. You can tell her that, as a wine connoisseur, as you certainly are, as far as she is concerned, being English and ex-public school."

"So this is how you spend your life here? Are these little squabbles your passion now?" Somewhere he felt sorry for her, but what he said sounded sarcastic. He didn't really mean it that way.

"They are not really 'my passion,' but I have to do it. Otherwise I would think too much about Robert. You just told me that I think about Robert too much, didn't you?"

"Why don't you want to think about Robert, if everything is OK?" he challenged her. "There wouldn't be any harm in it then."

"Oh, don't pretend, Paul." She was suddenly angry. With him, Robert or with herself? "You have already noticed that everything is not OK. It's just like Nicola's kitchen. Everything looks as if it is OK. I don't want to have time to think. When I only start to analyze his behavior, I immediately begin to doubt, whether he loves me at all. Because long ago I lost already any doubt that he had ever loved me as much as I loved him. And that is my problem, because I had always promised myself that I would never love any man more than he loved me. The one who loves more suffers more at the time of parting." She stopped abruptly as if she was frightened even to talk about it. "Hadn't we better go from here? Looking down into the distance always makes me contemplate my life. We should see Nicola and laugh a little at her." But she couldn't stop herself from finishing her previous thought, as if she wanted to cast it from her mind, to get rid of it forever. "Because parting is unavoidable. If not by separation, it would happen by death." And she shivered suddenly, leant against him and kissed him unexpectedly. "Yes, you are right; I think about it too much."

He didn't have time to reciprocate, still puzzled by her kiss as two boys approached them from behind, heading for the drinks trolley. One of the teenagers was a son of Nicola's third husband from his second marriage, if Paul correctly remembered the complicated relationships in these modern American families.

The boys didn't notice Natalie and Paul standing in the dark, and they probably hoped they would not be seen as they got their quiet drink.

"Hi, John," called Natalie. And Paul saw that he was right in his suspicion of the reason why the boys were there, because the taller one jumped suddenly, as if caught red handed. "Hi, John, don't worry." She gave him a friendly smile. "Have you seen Tricia lately?"

"Yes, hello, I've just seen her." He calmed down quickly and smiled back while answering in the manner expected from the well-behaved, public school teenager. "She is with us down by the pool. Shall I give her a message?"

"No, thank you," she said and immediately, contradicting herself, added: "Yes, just tell her, please, that her mother loves her very much and we haven't seen you here," she added in a conspiratorial tone. Paul saw that she looked much happier now and much more attuned to reality.

"Shall we go dancing?" she proposed, just as Paul was about to suggest the same.

So they went toward the parquet floor, leaving the two boys to the trolley. Paul was looking forward to dancing with Natalie, to holding her in his arms. But just as they were approaching the crowd of dancers, Nicola's voice grabbed them from behind.

"I've been looking for you two everywhere. Have you forgotten about our little party upstairs?"

It was definitely Nicola's loud, domineering voice. Paul didn't even need to turn for confirmation, and in fact he didn't really want to turn. But what could he do? Nicola expected good manners from him, a man who had been in Eton, the only English public school they had heard of here. And, after all, he was with Natalie, and it would be an affront to her best friend.

"Where have you been hiding yourselves?" asked Nicola, winking knowingly to Natalie.

"He was sufficient for the first hour of your party," said Natalie, smiling, "but now I was already getting bored with him, so we were going to see you and your exciting proposals for having a good time."

This was probably the answer Nicola had expected, because she appreciated it by embracing Natalie and patting her on the back.

Why is she lying? We were going dancing, not to see this garish chatterbox, thought Paul, but he chose to say nothing.

"So you are bored with Paul after one hour?" asked Nicola with deliberately exaggerated surprise, which promisingly suggested: I would not be bored with you, Paul, after an hour.

"Maybe I expect too much from a man," jokingly added Natalie "and obviously no one can be like the prince from my girlish dreams."

"Why not?" asked Nicola challengingly, "I'm also still looking for my Mr. Right." And she smiled provocatively at Paul. "The most important is to believe that he exists somewhere."

"Is that your reason for having so many relationships?" asked Natalie ironically. "Because you are still looking for the perfect man. It sounded as if she wanted to have it confirmed. And the confirmation came as expected:

"Yes, exactly," admitted Nicola, smiling again to Paul. "This is how I explain it to all my lovers. Actually, this is the reason why they are all competing with each other. To be the best. To be my Mr. Right." And she laughed confidently at her joke. Now she lowered her voice, as if she wanted to confide something, and added in even more cheeky tone:

"The most important is that they know that no one possesses me completely. Even my husband. All men are conquerors, and as soon as they conquer something they start looking for new conquests."

"That's why you have Bobby and others before him? So your husband won't take you for granted?" asked Natalie. Her voice was omniscient as well as disbelieving.

"And what did you think?" Nicola answered defiantly again. "Maybe you thought that because I prefer his penis to Andrew's. Andrew is my husband," she quickly snapped this explanation towards Paul. But he didn't want it. He would prefer not to be addressed. He was much happier when he believed that two women were oblivious of his existence. He felt embarrassed being present at this conversation.

"May I do prefer Bobby's," Nicola continued, as if she were thinking aloud. "Maybe I really do," she repeated as she laughed carelessly at her memory. "But that is not the main reason." And she suddenly became serious and started to explain. "Bobby is twenty years younger than me, the same age as Andrew's secretary. So when Andrew sees that young boys prefer me to his secretary, he would look silly in his own eyes if he preferred her. Logical, isn't it?"

"Yes," they both answered almost simultaneously and so automatically that they looked at each other and smiled.

"I really admire your logic," repeated Natalie.

Was it sarcasm in her voice or only jealousy? asked Paul of himself but didn't have time to analyze it, because Nicola was talking about him just now. Again in her challenging voice:

"Didn't you have the same reason for bringing Paul here?" And she turned to Paul again. "You don't mind our talking so personally in front of you?" And, not waiting for his answer, continued to Natalie. "You don't have any secrets in front of Paul, do you? As I don't in front of Bobby."

"You are right," answered Natalie. "I don't have any, I guess." And she frowned in quick glance at Paul as if asking him not to protest. It seems that I'm going to play the role of Nicola's Bobby for this evening, he thought, and at the same moment he realized that he found it amusing and suddenly started to enjoy the conversation. Americans are so sure of themselves in drawing assumptions, he thought, and everything seems to be so straight and simple for them. Let's listen and learn something more about this simplicity. Also, he went on in justifying his behavior internally, it would be stupid to miss an opportunity to learn something more about psychology of women, such a fashionable topic nowadays. The last sentence nearly slipped out of his mouth.

"You really think I have everything so logically arranged?" asked Nicola again, as if she wanted to get their approval once more. They nodded while she continued: "I suppose it's true right now, but if you knew me before! Oh! I was so completely hopeless. In logic, math, life, anything. Nobody knows about it here. Even Bobby I don't know why I want to tell you about it just now. I must be drunk, I suppose."

"Don't tell us; if you are not sure, you should," said Natalie, but Paul knew that she really wanted to hear it.

"No, no! I want to tell you. I have to tell somebody about it!" protested Natalie hotly. "I can hardly believe it was me; the hopeless stupid creature I used to be." She drank some champagne from her glass. "You know," she started again, "I used to live in Liverpool, England." I thought so, went through Paul's brain, but he didn't want to interrupt.

"So, when I used to live in Liverpool, I was one of those battered English wives there. The ones who are so hopeless that they are convinced that it is their fault when their husbands beat them." Her voiced quivered and broke. Her hand shook as she nervously finished her champagne. "I was so hopeless," she continued. "I couldn't do anything well enough to please him. So he had to beat me, even though, he used to say, he hated doing it to me." She laughed cynically. "I was so hopeless! And I still thought that I could fight off his violence by my gentleness, by loving him."

"And did you? Did you? So what happened?" asked Natalie impatiently, while Nicola was pouring herself another glass of champagne.

Paul wanted to signal to Natalie not to show how much she was involved, unless she wanted Nicola to guess that she was once in a similar situation and gossip about it all over Beverly Hills.

"So what happened?" Nicola repeated Natalie's question. "He did the best thing he could possibly do." And she paused again, as if waiting for further questions, and when they didn't come as quickly as she expected, she said: "Yes, he did the best thing he ever did in his whole life. He died!" And she smiled casually, as she had done yesterday when talking about wine and flowers. "But at that time," and she smiled again, only a little sad or pondering. "But at that time," she repeated, "it was the end of the world for me. I tried to kill myself three or four times. Good job that somebody always found me before it was too late. Otherwise," and she looked around, "I wouldn't be here now, in this most beautiful place in the world. And I wouldn't be myself, so happy, cool and logical as I am now. Like a different person. Like in a different life."

"Maybe you needed those experiences to become so cool and logical," said Natalie.

"Oh, yes, you're right," agreed Nicola. It seemed as if she wanted to add something, but she didn't. Instead she suddenly reversed into the usual flirtatious Nicola and said quickly, "we can't talk about it just now, because I see one of my battered men approaching. I promised them that we would have a little sex party upstairs before Andrew comes. "She now spoke very quickly, as if she wanted to explain before the man reached them. "I call them my 'battered men' because I really batter them; not physically, of course, but if s still battering. I like the feeling that I can do with Bobby whatever I want and he will still love me the same. I suppose I get pleasure from moral cruelty as my first husband did from beating me. Now I'm the one who is in the control, and I love it that way. I have power . . ."

"I can imagine how you feel," exclaimed Nicola spontaneously. "I would love to have power over a man I love! Power to change him!" Paul knew that she was thinking about Robert, for her eyes had a dreamlike quality again.

"Should we want to change the people we love, or accept them with all their faults?" asked Paul to provoke some discussion: He didn't want to see Natalie withdraw again.

"That's a good question for the younger generation," said Nicola, putting her arm on the broad shoulder of a blond, tall, young and handsome typical Californian who had just approached them. She didn't need to introduce him after the way they looked at each other. "What do you think about it, Bobby?" She dragged him straight into the conversation.

"Are we talking about love again?" he asked with rising criticism in his voice. But he withdrew it immediately under Nicola's threatening glare. "I don't mean 'again' because I'm bored by the subject. Oh, no! Absolutely not!" he exclaimed and, probably to demonstrate his enthusiasm, he lifted Nicola up in his athletic arms and kissed her cheek loudly and passionately. "I love talking about love," he said, putting her down back to the floor. "In fact, all the young generation, as Nicola calls us, love talking about love and love being in love as well. Frankly, some of the older generation I know," and he looked at Nicola with a mischievous smile, "especially those who want to be young forever, also love being in love."

"Oh, Bobby . . ." started Nicola.

"I'm not talking about Nicola, "she continued, clarifying jokingly, "because she always introduces herself as six months younger than me, in heart. But I don't mind her little lies. I still love her." And he squeezed her against his broad chest. "Let's dance, baby. Don't waste time."

The same thought had been in Paul's mind for some time already. But his problem was that he didn't know how to dance to these Latin American rhythms. So he just put his hand round Natalie's waist, letting her know that he was ready to protect her from these aggressive Californian males, who had already joined Nicola and Bobby in their dancing.

Natalie didn't protest at his gesture, but she looked at Nicola and Bobby, moving sensually to music, and said sadly: "Yes, love is the best medicine for everything."

Nicola was now again close to them, in the subsequent dancing position. She probably heard the word "love," or maybe it was constantly on her mind, for she shouted in their ears over the music: "Enjoy love as long as you have it." And she was again grabbed by Bobby, who bent her over to the floor in the following classical ballroom position, saying with exaggerated passion: "It's God's blessing to be able to love."

But he looked more like a demon than an angel, to Paul at least. Maybe to Natalie as well, because she suddenly said:

"When you are in love, you are oblivious to faults."

"Oh, no, not always!" protested Nicola, who was just passing them in another complicated movement (to Paul anyway). "I can see faults in a man I love. And I like to correct them," she staccatoed aggressively towards Bobby.

And afterwards regret the change you made," he finished her sentence, laughing domineeringly and squeezing her in his arms as they moved into another dancing position. "You remember when you made me grow a beard?" he asked, but she ignored it. She stopped dancing and now stood next to Natalie. She looked as she was musing on some idea.

"Why can I see so many faults in any man I'm with?" she asked herself aloud and came with the answer immediately, as it had been ready in her mind for sometime. "Maybe because I've learned that it was wrong not to see them in the one I told you about."

"Who was so lucky? Who was so lucky?" insisted Bobby with childish impatience, but it was clear that he wasn't desperate for an answer as much as he was desperate for his dancing with Nicola.

"Oh, yes, it is wrong not seeing men's faults," agreed Natalie. "But isn't that real love?"

Nobody answered. Bobby was moving sensuously, as if the music were in his veins. He seemed to be in a touching mood as well. His hands were all over Nicola, inciting her to move to the music with him.

"I sometimes think," said Natalie again, "that we not only can't see the faults in the person we love, but we even interpret them as virtues." Paul noticed her habitual bitter smile whenever she talked about Robert. "Once I believed that the man I loved was a courageous scientist experimenting on himself with a new drug to help the future population when he was smoking hashish."

"It definitely helps in populating the world, "interrupted Bobby facetiously." We know how some organs grow rapidly after smoking hashish," and he winked towards Paul, obviously sure that it was common knowledge amongst men. "Apropos hashish," his tone now changed to one of a child complaining about the injustice of its mother, "Nicola promised us a quiet "sex party" upstairs before Andrew comes back, and we are all smoking up there and waiting and she is still downstairs. So Robert sent me down here to get you."

"Oh yes, I've forgotten all about it, I'm sorry," exclaimed Nicola.

"And I've forgotten what did I come for, while dancing with you," admitted Bobby, rubbing Nicola against himself.

"Let's go, then," Natalie unexpectedly approved the idea. Did she miss Robert already, or did she want to see what he was up to this time? thought Paul.

"OK, let's go then," agreed Nicola. "But we, girls, go first," she added. "Nobody need know that we have a separate party going on upstairs."

"I call it hypocrisy," Bobby teased her again, "but I still love you. It can't be hypocrisy, it can't be a fault, if it comes from you. You are so perfect."

"I know I am," said she, and the "girls" were off giggling and rushing like teenagers, pushing through the dancing crowd.

All this was slowly getting on Paul's nerves. This abandon of Bobby, all this loud and demanding new generation, so lucky in getting what they want . . .

"We can follow the girls by now."

Bobby patted Paul intimately on the shoulders and gripped him with his athletic arm in what he would probably have regarded as a friendly gesture, pulling him towards the house, towards a wide open terrace door. "We can follow them now, just about. Unless you want to dance for a moment?" he asked. "It's quite a good tango. I like tango. If you want." He looked as if he had another of his great ideas. "I can show you a new position we learned in our ballroom dancing classes. Nicola and I are taking ballroom dancing lessons. It's great fun. And Nicola loves dancing. You saw it yourself: I came down here looking for her to take her upstairs to show her my other abilities, you know," and Bobby again patted Paul's shoulder intimately, "but, as you saw, she was only interested in dancing. Let's go" he added harshly. "I can remind her of my other abilities before Andrew comes back." And he ran towards the terrace. Paul followed him through the terrace door, into the house and straight upstairs. "It's such fun to be in love," cried Bobby vigorously. "But I don't need to tell you that. You must have the same sort of fun with Natalie?"

Paul didn't have time to protest even if he wanted to, because Bobby was already pointing out another assumption:

"You know the worst problem most Englishmen have is their inability to love. Or it could be their inability to show their emotions. Yes. Yes, it would be that," he answered himself. "They don't even know how much fun is. missing from their lives because of this handicap. Not to mention their wives for whom life must be a misery; in that cold country with their cold husbands."

"It isn't that bad," protested Paul. "We would have a higher divorce rate if women felt that miserable. Somehow California has the highest rate of divorce."

"Oh, no, you're not giving me that crap about statistics! Where can your English housewives go if they have no job, no love but plenty of children? They have no choice. Our girls here are really free; when they stay with you, you can tell it's for love, not because they have no choice. Isn't that more honest?"

"It sounds like it," agreed Paul. There was no point in discussing it now, and above all they were already upstairs, in front of "Nicola's Games Room," as it was announced on the door.

Bobby opened it without knocking. The room was darkish, lit only with candles, spread unevenly here and there. There was plenty of smoke from hashish and possibly opium; Paul couldn't tell. It was so dark that he was unable to recognize any of the occupants. They were lying or sitting on heaps of colorful pillows which had been thrown everywhere around the floor, covered by Persian carpets of all sizes and colors, thrown unevenly on top of each other.

The only person he recognized instantly, maybe because he was expecting to find him here, was Robert. And he looked as Paul would have expected to find him in these circumstances; the leader of the show. Like in the old days in Cambridge, when they would entertain themselves by performing masquerades. There could be no doubt about it that the place Robert was occupying was the center of the stage. The candles were less scattered there and actually formed a sort of circle surrounding a shiny golden-reddish tent which was undoubtedly made of silk, because it emitted that mysterious luster of opulence which only real silk can give. Robert's visir or pasha-like dress gave the same luminosity of eastern wealth in its soft folds, where the yellow became more golden than yellow and the red more purple than red.

He was sitting proudly on a golden stool in front of the open tent, and all the lights in the room seemed to be suddenly reflected in the diamond brooch on his turban, when he turned his erect head towards the newcomers. Paul was blinded by that brightness for the moment. When he regained his visual ability, another sudden light's reflection came to his eyes from a mirrored wall. This was because Robert had turned his head towards these mirrors (which, as Paul learned later, hid a door to the dressing room which had just opened) and the reflected light of the candles in Robert's brooch shone back towards Paul from there.

Nicola came from behind that mirror, also dressed in red and yellow, which, as Paul admitted to himself, meshed these Turkish surroundings perfectly. He realized now that he liked masquerades even more than he thought he did. The tone in which she spoke again reminded him of Cambridge and of masquerades organized there.

"Natalie says," informed Nicola, walking towards Robert in the slow, provocative movement of a harem dancing girl, "that she is not getting changed until she knows what this sex-play will be about." She smiled at Robert rebelliously, but coquettishly. "And I agree with her. So can you tell us what is the idea for tonight?"

"Oh, don't ask, woman!" said Robert impatiently, just like a visir would do to one of his women. "You will never have any fun if you know too much. You'd better show these two new slaves to their changing room so we can start afterwards." It was ordered with pointing at Paul and Bobby, in a very proper for the occasion, domineering manner. Robert didn't seem to be as drunk as Paul expected to find him after what he had seen him drinking downstairs.

"But how are we going to start?" Nicola insisted. "Because if you think that Natalie and I will play subservient little women again you are quite mistaken. And, anyway, we have a very good idea for tonight. Everybody listen, please," she was undoubtedly taking Robert's role from him just now. Paul could always tell when Robert was annoyed. Nobody else noticed. Everybody's attention was on Nicola. "First, all the men have to undress and prepare their erect penises for surveying. Next, the . . ."

Next the door opened sharply, into Paul's back. He almost fell from the force.

"Hello, darling. Hello everybody. Sorry for being late for the party." At the door stood a tall, well built, well dressed yet insignificant looking man.

"Oh, hello, darling," cried back Nicola. "I thought you would be even later." She ran towards him, ostentatiously showing her love and attention. They were strangely mismatched, but Paul has no doubt that it was Nicola's husband, Andrew.

"You don't want to study conjugal greetings," whispered Bobby into Paul's ear, pulling him out of the room.

They went downstairs and out to the garden. Paul didn't feel well. His adrenalin level was going dramatically up. He didn't know whether it was from the alcohol or from the expectation of the sex party. He wanted to be with Natalie right now, but at the same time he perceived guilt and regret towards this feeling. He envied Bobby his careless, free personality which enabled him to boast with a totally clean conscience about loving a married woman.

It was a little cooler here down on the terrace, now, just after sunset. He took a deep breath as he was taught in his stress release classes. Multicolored electric lights were already on around the dancing floor, over the tables and down in the garden. Everything looked surprisingly jolly and so unrealistic to Paul that he felt as though he had suddenly been mistakenly put into the set of a Fellini film, where everything seemed to be exaggerated, the colors, the music people's acting, their gestures and voices. He was glad to have Bobby next to him; Bobby who seemed to be so at home here, even now, when they were pulled along by the revelling crowd, who were clapping and shouting to them in Italian, words probably connected with the Tarantella which was being danced all over the parquet floor. Bobby was clapping and stamping so well that one of the Italian girls pulled him into the dancing circle. Paul stood and watched. The Tarantella was being performed so professionally that it reminded him of a folk performance on an Italian town square during his holiday, when, as a small boy, he had looked on from the corner of the square, with his little, hot hand, shaking from excitement, in the cold, decisive hand of his mother.

The memory was so tangible that suddenly he sensed the cold, decisive hand in his own. He shook off his dream, but the cold hand not only remained in its place, but even somehow tightened around his fingers.

"Why are you shaking so much?" asked Natalie. He relaxed. It was only Natalie. He repeated her name aloud:

"Natalie!" All his present problems connected with that name reappeared sharply. "I've just been thinking about you," he said, "and how difficult it is to love a married woman." That is probably what Bobby would say, he thought. Nothing hidden. No pretence. Going straight to the point. He decided to apply this same technique, for this evening at least, and if he should go too far he could always say tomorrow that he was drunk and didn't remember what he had been doing.

"The worst time I have now is lying in your spare bedroom and imagining what you are doing with Robert before going to sleep. Maybe you are undressing in front of him, maybe you're having a bath together and he is carrying you naked afterwards." He couldn't talk anymore as he experienced the same physical pain of envy that he felt every night in bed.

She also looked as though it was painful for her.

"It isn't like that! It's not like that at all!" she cried out. Her voice was harsh, her eyes large and angry. "I would love it to have like that! But it isn't, and I know it'll never be like that!" And she smiled, her usual bitter smile, which Paul knew so well, always when she talks about Robert.

"Every night I lie in my bedroom and cry. We use two bedrooms now, haven't you noticed? The bathroom between them is the only area that is shared. Sometimes after our regular evening quarrel he rapes me there, to establish his superiority, when he runs out of other arguments. Let's dance; it's better if we don't talk about it." But he knew that she couldn't stop now. "Even being here makes me feel upset; seeing all these lucky women, loved and admired by their husbands. And what about me? I'm not worse looking or less intelligent, so why?"

Paul felt that it would be the right time to propose, right now.

"You know, you can still have all that. In England. With me."

But she even didn't want to talk about it:

"Stop it, please," she said sadly. "It makes me even more upset. Or maybe, not. I don't know. I don't think I know anything for sure any more, except that I'm unable to leave Robert! Even now when I have no hope left that he will ever change. Let's dance, forget it!" But she didn't move and started again in a bitter, desperate tone; "I despise myself for not being strong enough to leave him, and I despise myself for not being strong enough to change him. If you don't respect yourself, how could you expect others to respect you? I'm falling again into that pattern of thinking of battered wives, who justify the way their husbands treat them," she noticed it soberly and objectively but immediately afterwards allowed herself to retreat into even bigger desperation: "I'm good for nothing. I can't even keep my child at home, because I don't trust my husband. Where is she anyway? Where is my child now?" she cried out suddenly, in what Paul thought was an unexpectedly strong panic.

"Remember, before we went upstairs, she was still by the swimming pool, with the other kids," said Paul in a quiet voice, to appease her. "It's nothing to panic about," he added, as he pulled her closer. "Let's dance, please."

It was so good holding her in his arms, moving rhythmically to the music. He didn't want to stop it just yet, but Natalie pushed him away. One look at her and it was obvious that nothing except Tricia's well being could now be allowed to enter her mind.

"It's easy to say don't panic." She had already stopped dancing and was pushing her way through the crowd, toward the side of the garden, with the swimming pool at the back. Paul reluctantly followed her across the floor.

"I always have this feeling when something happens to Tricia," she was telling him while rushing out of the parquet. She took her shoes off now and ran barefoot on the sharp pebbles of the alley. "It suddenly struck me while we were dancing. I wish I didn't have this telepathy with her. Oh, my God, I feel she is in danger!" she cried out, running faster and faster, Paul hardly managed to keep up with her. He sensed as if Natalie's feeling of potential danger were gradually implanting into him. He wanted to help, to prevent. Tricia was such a sweet, little girl. And she was so precious to Natalie.

"Please, God, let nothing happen to her!" Natalie breathed out the words which Paul was just about to say aloud but didn't, frightened that he might aggravate her even more.

She had the rhythmic breath of a runner. She must be jogging every morning here, like most of them, came to his mind very improperly, as he thought later, since he should have been thinking only about Tricia. Maybe it was a self-defensive thought, since I started worrying about her too much, he thought.

She wasn't at the swimming pool. They learned there that her father had taken her back home, just five or ten minutes ago.

"Her father?" confirmed Natalie, and the words seemed to choke her.

"Yes, her father," repeated the youngster.

"They went by taxi," added another young boy, "because her father was quite drunk." And he smiled as if remembering something funny.

"Thank you," said Natalie in a cool, controlled voice. "Thank you, and have a good day. Bye."

Paul was surprised that she could control herself so well, at the swimming pool, where children were watching, but also later while they were walking towards the car park. Walking, not running anymore. Now he wanted to run. He looked at her in disbelief again. And this was when he noticed the sort of resignation in her posture. No, it was more than that! He caught himself taking a second look at her. Her posture conveyed total apathy!

The car park wasn't far. She went straight to her car, automatically, like a mechanical doll. Paul was worried for a moment that she was unable to drive. But she was, and they drove home calm and collected.

"I knew it had to happen sooner or later," she said while she was parking the car, in front of the house, so close that it nearly touched the marble steps. And she was already out. Paul had to rush again, to catch up with her. She went straight upstairs. Straight to Tricia's bedroom. Marching like a Gestapo officer in a war film. And there they were: her Tricia and her Robert, together. Both naked, and on the bed! Tricia lying straight, rigid, as if paralyzed, by their unexpected entry or by Robert, who was sitting over her, on her stomach, his knees against her breasts, his penis in front of her eyes, erect.

"See, how big . . ." boasting pride in Robert's voice.

"Oh, yes, she can see it." It was Natalie. "She can see it very well."

Robert didn't move, but his whole body stiffened suddenly. The picture was so static that Paul felt for a moment as if he was in some sort of perverted wax figure's museum.

"She can see it equally well," continued Natalie, "as she saw it when she was three years old and it was on the level of her eyes while you were dancing naked in front of her. You remember? You made her stay and look and touch!" She was talking more slowly and more calmly with each word, until her tone gradually became one of those which psychotherapists use to their clients.

"Now you had better come with us. It's late. The child has to sleep."

"Oh, Mammy, oh, Mammy," Tricia suddenly cried out. It sounded like a great relief of a paralyzed throat. "Oh, Mammy, how good that you came." She still couldn't move, because Robert continued sitting on her stomach his penis between her breasts towards her face.

"Be quiet child," said Natalie, still with that slow-paced voice. "Come with us, Robert. You know, you can't do anything else right now."

Her voice was so cool, so controlled, as if this scene didn't involve her at all, as if these two people were not the only people she loved.

She talked calmly, in the upper class accent, Paul knew, she used with her clients. It appeared to Paul as if she had rehearsed the role many times. Was it expected? went through his mind. He wanted to make this situation easier for all of them.

"Shall I go?" he asked.

Robert's protest came nearly at the same time as Natalie's. She was maybe a moment quicker, with fright in her voice, as if this idea terrified her.

"Oh, no, no! You stay here, please." She stressed "please"; a word she rarely used.

Robert's voice was shaking and very different from the one Paul knew of him through all those years.

"Oh, no, no! You stay here, old chap! You've seen me already on so many different roles." He seemed to need to talk for talking sake, because gradually, as he was doing it, he was slowly regaining his usual half-cheeky, half-facetious tone of voice. "Somebody has to give Tricia some anatomy lessons. And it's better if it comes from me than from some healthy and vulgar American bullock . . . Nowadays with AID's around we even can't be sure if he would be a healthy little bullock." And he laughed at his joke looking around for applause; obviously feeling back in control. "We are still admitting his dominance and helping him to restore his dignity. Why is that?" Paul wasn't sure what shocked him more; that thought or the facts in front of his eyes.

# Natalie's Diary 7

## Saturday, 5 September (next year)

I predicted it! I knew it before! I had this premonition already many years ago, when Tricia was only three and her father was dancing naked in front of her eyes. Already then I knew that sooner or later he would try to rape her. Already then I detected in him the rapist's psyche. And that psyche kept revealing itself from time to time throughout all our life together. Especially during our discussions and quarrels, while if he any time lacked a logical argument he would immediately use his rapist's power as a convincing, final one.

I think that the rapist psyche develops mainly in men who are frustrated and full of complexes, in men who are incapable of acquiring power in any other way than by rape, and in whom acquisition of power is the dominating force in life.

Yes, it fits; it even explains what happened today! So Robert would probably be even "entitled" to be frustrated because Nicola had stolen from him the power, the ability to control people, at that party upstairs. Yes, that's what happened. And on top of it he also had the right to feel frustrated because of sex, because I haven't slept with him for nearly a week. Yes, it would be an English court's justification of the poor fellow. And eventually it would be all my fault because I haven't slept with him for nearly a week so that English judge, Harold Castle, would say: "the wife's lack of sexual appetite would lead to sexual problems for a healthy young husband." I'll never forget Sir Harold summing up in the High Court on October twenty-first nineteen hundred and eighty-eight, when he tried to justify the rape of a twelve-year-old girl by her stepfather with the fact that his wife was pregnant and "pregnant ladies are naturally not very receptive to their husbands."

Am I starting to think in the terms of "that senile old fool" (as the mother of that twelve-year-old girl called him), in that most backward of civilized countries regarding women's rights? Anything for justifying Robert.

Objectively I haven't even got the slightest doubt that what Robert did tonight was a crime, but at the same time I have tried at any price to justify the criminal, because the criminal is Robert. Love is the most unjust, the most biased judge. It doesn't reckon with right and wrong. It reckons with "being with him or without him." And in my case for "being with him," I'm still ready to do anything. And it frightens me in its perverse obscenity, in its masochistically suicidal tendencies. Until now I have always been too afraid to admit how much I'm still ready to do, to forget and to justify, to be able to make sure that my final judgement would arrive at the verdict "to be with him."

How can I even think about that sort of verdict?! It is ignoring the child! The shock she has gone through. This child for whom I decided to stay in the West, missing my country so much. The child for whom I had to suffer humiliation of dancing in German nightclubs and for whose stable future I sold myself to David. For this child I've established, so-called normal family life with Robert, later with David and now with Robert again, only to demolish everything with that verdict.

This verdict means exile for the child from normal family life forever. This verdict will put her into a boarding school, with as limited possibility of seeing her parents as possible. Both of her parents. Because how will I be able to look into her eyes after that verdict? How can I tell her that I forgave her father for his crime?

Some people boast that they are governed by, as they call it, superior morality, or in other words, loyalty towards the person they live with: husband, son, mother. They boast that they conceal that person's crime . . . Would it be right to hide his crime?

Oh, my god, I see that all my morality is going berserk! All my moral values tangled. All my internal judgment seems to be lost. Or maybe I just don't want to permit the thought that according to my old morality, I should kill him for what he has done to me and my child.

Oh, no, never! I love him! I can't even think like that! I love him so much! Should we be allowed to forget our moral values for the price of saving a loved one? In fact isn't it saving my loved one or just selfishly saving my own love? My idea of being in love? And my life. Because without him my life has no purpose, no sense.

You forgot about the child! What about your loyalty towards the child? If we are talking about loyalty, to whom should a woman be more loyal; towards her husband or towards her child?

# Chapter 8

## *Back In London*

He couldn't believe his eyes! It shocked him! It was a pleasant shock, of course, but still a shock and he never liked shocks whatever kind they were. But at the same time it was also like a realization of his dreams. Suddenly he realized that he had imagined a similar scene so many times that now he wasn't sure if it still wasn't one of his dreams about her.

She was standing at the door like the very first time when she came to his office. Even her dress was similar. "She is always in red" quickly went through his mind, and he just started considering whether not to pinch himself, in order to be sure he wasn't dreaming, when Sue rushed into the room, full of apologies and explanations.

Now he learned that Sue was not allowed to announce Natalie, that Sue was pushed back into her chair by Natalie's firm voice and her order: "Don't even get up, Sue, I have to surprise him'/ as Natalie stormed through Sue's office. There was no time to stop her, to intercept her. She was so sure of her rights. He knew Sue didn't like strong women, even though she claimed to be a feminist.

"Thank you, Sue, thank you," he said. "It's all right, you can go." He couldn't stop her talking, and he wanted so much to be left alone with Natalie.

"Shall I bring tea?" It was obvious that Sue wanted to postpone her departure. Probably nearly as strongly as Paul she longed to find out what had brought Natalie here.

"No, thank you, Sue. It would do. You can go." And with these words Natalie gently pushed her out of the room and closed the door.

They were alone at last, and Paul found himself already next to her, keeping her hand, kissing it and leading her towards the less formal part of the room with a leather sofa in the corner of it. He realized that he had never acted so fast and so positively in all his life. He felt like somebody else or himself in his dreams about her. But he found that he was still holding her hand and it was warm and soft, real flesh, so it couldn't be a dream.

She kissed his cheek now, looking pleased and amused at his enthusiastic greeting.

"Yes, it's me. Don't worry, I'm not going to run away, so don't squeeze my hand so much." She was smiling at him with the smile of his mother when she had visited him for the first time in his boarding school. He remembered that he had torn her dress by squeezing it in his hand. He was suddenly angry with himself and with this memory. He was a grown up man now, so he should be able to control his feelings. He let her hand go. He sat up straight on the sofa, took a big breath to prevent the stutter which he still could expect at times of great emotion, and asked as calmly as he could.

"When did you come to London? And is it for long?"

"I came just now. I'm straight from the airport," she rushed with answers. "I have to talk to you. I don't know for how long I'll be here. Maybe forever."

He couldn't keep control. He couldn't act formally and coolly, especially after her last sentence . . . He grabbed her hand again and pulled it towards his lips. She seemed to approve this time. Her smile became softer and somehow sad.

"I'll tell you everything now," she said. "I didn't write about it in my letters because I always hoped that it might change so there was no point in alarming you. "She looked at him with a really caring smile. Just like he wanted her to look. "First, immediately after you and Tricia left, we had a "period of his dreamland", when, after his hashish and alcohol, half jokingly, he would paint for me his vision of an ideal family. It means, when our family would be ideal for him. He saw the three of us: he, myself and Tricia, on the carport in front of an open fire, enjoying joint sex, joint smoking, joint drink . . . This period I called "negotiations," because he tried to negotiate his right to both of his women. At this period he was very attentive and very loving towards me. It was apparent that he was very determined about achieving positive results from these negotiations. But I couldn't permit that, and Tricia stayed at boarding school. So then the second period started, "His devotion to work." He started staying longer at work. At least that was what I was told. When he came he smelled of alcohol, hashish and perfume, and always tried to rape me, to prove that he hadn't slept with other women. But knowing his potency, it wouldn't be proof anyway. Once, during his evenings at work, I met him in Nicola's, when I paid her an unexpected visit. He watched her indulging in sex with her big afghan dog. It was work, I was told. He needed this experience for his next scripts. It made me sick, and I didn't let him come near me that night, so he beat and raped me, pretending to be a dog, playfully imitating a dog's noises and doing it the way they do it . . . It was when I realized just how sadistic a nature he had. When I saw the amount of pleasure he drew from my terror and disgust, I tried to conceal it and lay like a stone, for not giving him more satisfaction." Her eyes were empty when they met with Paul's just now.

"I'm sorry," he said, but she didn't seem to hear it, continuing her monologue:

"I had my period that night, and the sight of blood always made him more wild. That night it made him completely crazy. When he was lying exhausted afterwards he said that he never had such a great orgasm before, that I'm the woman of his life, and that loves me so much that he would kill anybody who would want to take me from him and that he would kill me if I ever tried to leave him. "She suddenly woke up as from a trance, squeezed his hands in hers since they were there during all this time and whispered in terrified voice: "He must never find out that I'm here, that I'm here with you . . ." "Yes, yes, of course," started Paul, but she was again back in the past: "I know, it was that night when I had this dream for the first time. This dream which comes back again and again. There is that last drop of red wine falling into a huge glass, which is overflowing and a cascade of red wine is spouting now and pouring down onto white marble steps, pushing down a small female figure struggling to stay on these suddenly slippery and dirty red steps. It's such a fight that I always wake up sweating, and it was never clear to me if I managed to hold onto the step or not and if it was wine or blood pouring over me and pushing me down. And this dream comes back again and again. I know, it's not normal. You don't need to tell me that. And that is what I'm worried about, because, what my struggle can symbolize? It only can be the struggle to stay alive or to stay insane. The latter I'm more afraid of. And, I'm so afraid of him. "She squeezed the lapels of Paul's jacket in her hands and pressed her hand against Paul's chest like a child looking for protection.

Paul was proud of his reaction. He embraced her gently and caressingly stroked her hair. Like a real man. Like the responsible protector she was looking for. He could say he felt exceptionally good at that moment if only he could ignore the feeling of fear which she had already imparted in him.

"And I'm so afraid of him," Natalie repeated reflectively, "And this annoys me most, because I promised myself all those years ago that I would never let myself be afraid of him again. Will you talk to Sue, please, to make sure that he will never find out that I came here. It's very important. "She trembled, and her voice was shaking. "I shouldn't really come here. I should be in Spain by now. He thinks I'm already in Spain.

Oh, I didn't tell that did I? I'm sorry. You see, when I left him yesterday in New York I was going to Spain. But he is coming to London tomorrow. That's why I'm here. But he thinks I'm in Spain." She was talking fast, jumping from sentence to sentence, like in a high fever. Her breath short, irregular. "I love Spain. I can relax there. You remember Gaucin? That white village high in the mountains.

"Yes, I remember," Paul started slowly, hoping that this memory could relax her now. "Yes, I remember. We were looking from that village down on Gibraltar in the distance. Everything was so peaceful. It's already two years."

"It's only two years" Natalie corrected him. "But you are right. It seems like eternity." For a moment she looked rapt with this recollection. But she shook it off quickly. "It's where I'm supposed to meet him in about a week, when he has finished filming in London. I didn't tell you yet that Robert is coming here, did I?"

"Yes, you did," he wanted to say, but he stopped himself wisely. She didn't wait for his answer anyway.

"He is coming here tomorrow. That's why I'm here. But he mustn't know about it. I'm so afraid of him." She looked at Paul with those frightened eyes again. He felt he would do anything for her just now.

"It's OK. It' OK, Natalie. He will never know. I promise." Paul hurriedly stroked her hair again to calm her down, since he started to seriously worry about her condition.

"He is coming to discuss some sequences in the film he wrote a script for," Natalie explained, "and maybe take some part in producing it. It is supposed to take him a week and after that he was coming to see me in Spain. For "our next honeymoon," as he called it. But I don't want it. I have had enough of these honeymoons with him. And also, God knows what he wants to do to me in Spain. We will be alone there and, and . . . I'm so afraid of him." She pulled herself closer to Paul on the sofa. He protectively put his arm around her.

"I'm not supposed to, but I'm so afraid again," she cried out, shaking, "like at the time when I was last pregnant and he was threatening to kill me if I wouldn't have an abortion."

"What?" Paul couldn't control himself this time.

"Oh, yes, yes," she continued apathetically in a monotonous voice. "And he gave me all details of my death. How I would suffer before I'd died. And how nobody would know it was him. So I was so frightened that I had that abortion." She stopped for a moment. "But not now!" She said strongly, straightening herself up on the sofa. "But I'm not going to do it now. You see, I'm pregnant again," she added coolly, informatively, directly to Paul. "I know I didn't tell you that. I'm sorry, I'm rushing so much. I'm sorry," she repeated apologetically. She seemed to be back in reality, back in his office, looking straight into his eyes. "I know I should have written about it in my letters, but I was so afraid. I thought he would find out. Maybe he suspects anyway." She contemplated this thought for a moment. "Yes he might, because, you see, he is threatening me again. You see, he took me yesterday to his friend in New York who is a murderer. Why would he do it if not to threaten me again?" She looked at Paul, and a big question mark hung between them. Paul couldn't tell what answer she would prefer, and he didn't have one anyway.

"I know, I might exaggerate, "she started, probably reading it in his eyes. "And I know I'm getting crazy. You don't need to tell me that."

He thought for a moment that she was going to start analyzing her condition in an objective, professional manner, since the tone of her voice resembled now the one she used with her clients, but she withdrew that with a simple explanation:

"You see, I have nobody to talk to. And that is the problem. You are the only person I trust. That's why I'm here. I have to talk to somebody about it. And there is only you. They are all his friends. But you are also his friend. I don't know anything anymore. I'm getting mad. I'm sorry; I do trust you, Paul. I have to trust somebody anyway! But I know I shouldn't come here. I feel so guilty towards you. I know I used you, because of him. And I lost you, because of him. The only person I trust. The only friend I've got."

She was shaking all over, as if in a fever. Red cheeks, eyes glowing. Paul didn't know how to calm her down. He started to fear that she was heading towards a breakdown. "It is common knowledge nowadays that psychotherapists can also have a breakdown," he thought panicking.

"I'll get you some tea," he offered.

"No, no, thank you." she smiled as if he was joking. Her smile was quite natural. But her eyes still wild. "But maybe you have something stronger," she asked. "I know, I shouldn't drink." She added quickly as if to want to prevent his expected protest or her internal one. "I know I'm three months pregnant, but I don't think I can talk to you about it without a drink. And I have to talk. I really have to," she repeated with determination. "Now, when I've managed to start."

"OK, Natalie, I don't have anything here, in the office, but we can go somewhere for a drink. I'll cancel all my appointments for this afternoon." He was surprised that he could say it in such a normal voice. It was the first time that he had ever thought about cancelling any of his appointments, but it was for her. And she was in such a state. He felt like he was acting under the shock. No surprise" he thought "since he was receiving them one after the other. What was the last thing she said? That she was pregnant . . ." He felt he was not allowed to ask any questions. At least not now when she was like this. He knew that his responsibility now was to cool her down. To bring her back to the real world. So he said:

"Did you talk to your psychotherapist in L.A.?"

"No, I don't talk to anybody about Robert. They are all his friends, and I'm so frightened of them." And she moved back to the corner of the sofa, with her legs on it, knees drawn up to her chin, hands hugging them tightly so as to take as little space as possible, so as not to be seen in the dark corner of the sofa if anybody, (any of those friends of Robert) should come here now. Paul wasn't a psychotherapist, but even he saw that it was a persecution complex.

"I'm so frightened of them," she repeated. "They might tell Robert and—and—he would kill me. He has told me many times that he would kill me. I remember all the details. And he told me that nobody would even suspect it was him. He had so many clients who had murdered that he really knows how to do it. And what to do to avoid being caught. Do you have clients like that?" she asked suddenly, in a perfectly controlled voice, as casually as if they had just met at a party.

"Not really. I only defend when I believe a person is innocent."

"Robert defended anybody," Natalie interrupted him. "Robert still has these murderer friends, like the one in New York I've just started telling you about. So I might as well finish—"

"Wouldn't it be better—" interrupted Paul. He desperately wanted to help her, to make her think about something else. "Wouldn't it be better if we go out? You know, you can have a drink, we can walk around." He tried to tempt her. "Do you still love London so much?"

She seemed to be angry with him or with this question.

"You know I love London. You know I love walking here. I can walk here forever. I love the people here, I love everything about this city. But I feel like a foreigner here . . . again." She took a sad, melancholic, breath. "I don't know if London wants me anymore. If it can accept me with all my problems. I know there is something wrong with me. You have to listen to me, Paul! Please, just listen." She took his hand again, squeezed it in hers, but dropped it sooner than a moment; somehow she couldn't talk.

"Maybe you can find something to drink?" she asked. "I think Sue should have some champagne. In a respectable solicitor's office should be some champagne to celebrate won cases." Paul relaxed a little bit; she was her old self now, teasing him as usual.

"Oh, yes, Sue would have some champagne, but I remember you hate champagne."

"Oh, Paul. You remember that!" She looked touched by his consideration for her. She sat more comfortably. Seemed to be less tense now. "I can drink anything just now," she added.

She became even more her real self, at least the one Paul knew, after Sue left, leaving two bottles with them.

"To us!" Natalie toasted, with the same toast as always whenever they were drinking together. "It's so good to be with you again," she added warmly. But a second later she was different; her memories came back again.

"You see, it was on that night, when I had my period and he raped me so brutally, pretending to be a dog, and when I dreamt I was walking on those white marble stairs as though up to heaven, when suddenly this wine or blood, or dirt covered these stairs and forced me down, as though towards hell. You see, it was that night, when I first decided to kill him."

A shiver ran down Paul's spine, and a cold sweat covered his palms, which had suddenly turned icy. But its lasted only a moment. Much shorter than it should have, had that statement been a totally unexpected shock.

The realization of this physical fact, this physical reaction of his organism, came almost simultaneously with a sudden inner peace, which in us usually follows the receiving of long and impatiently awaited news. "No, it's impossible!" Paul didn't want to admit the thought to himself. How could it be true, that he was waiting for these words to pass between them.

"Yes, I want to kill him," Natalie repeated loudly, like somebody who wanted to hear one's own thoughts spoken aloud to experiment with and to get used to them. "Yes, it's true, Paul. And that's why I'm here, in London."

She stopped, as if she were awaiting his reaction. When he didn't say anything, didn't even move, she poured herself another glass of champagne and added slowly, as if trying to withdraw what she had just said:

"But I know that I never will be able to do it. I'd rather kill myself."

Paul was still unable to react, because he was still too absorbed in analyzing what had just happened to him. He was becoming more and more convinced that he had been expecting this moment for a long time and also that he had foreseen it as soon as he saw Natalie standing at the door. He now remembered that he had already then been worried about that unpredictable excess of energy which radiated from her. He realized now that it was due to this energy that her eyes were glowing so brightly and her body had been shaking feverishly throughout the whole of their meeting. It was this energy which was swelling within her, creating a pressure, as if it were too great for her small body, which was desperately fighting to accommodate the surplus and to prevent letting a danger out.

When he started listening again to what Natalie was saying, he realized that it was just what he had been thinking about.

"I feel that this internal, destructive power is getting stronger than me and that I'll soon be unable to hold it inside. It feels as if I'm fighting to hold down a champagne cork which has already been moved. You know it's impossible. Apropos, there's nothing left in that bottle. Open the second one, please," and she handed him her empty glass.

While he was struggling to open the bottle. (It's not so easy to start the cork going in the first place, Paul thought), she continued her monologue in a much cooler manner, somehow resembling her professional analysis of the possibility of danger and seeking ways of preventing it.

"Sometimes I'm frightened *of* myself. In fact, I don't know if it is myself. This voice inside my head, coaxing me to action. Probably more adequate would be to say I'm frightened *for* myself and also *for* Robert. This voice in my head, which determined for me that I should kill him, came for the first time on that night when he raped me in an animal fashion, but I think that unspoken desire for his death existed there already. I'm almost sure that it was already there at the moment when I saw him in bed on top of my child, that night in L.A. You remember, you saw it! Or maybe it was there even before that? Maybe already when I didn't want to have the abortion and I begged him to have a second child and to start normal family life devoted to children, etc. And he was not prepared, as he said, to sacrifice himself, his money, our love and privacy, for children. "The first one separated us strongly enough already,' he said." Now she drank a whole glass of champagne without taking her lips off the glass and added:

"I think it probably started even earlier, probably with that child, when he sent me with three-week-old Tricia to Poland, knowing that there were no legal agreements between those two countries. He said he is not a person who can take heavy responsibility. Somebody else's responsibility, as he called it. Because I shouldn't get pregnant if I didn't know how I would be able to feed that child. As if he weren't the father, I thought. So when, at the airport, he said that I could come back and try to live with him again, if I would dump the child in Poland, with my mother, I remember that this judicial voice inside my body said then: 'He is worse than an animal, because even animals care for their children.' I don't think this voice said then: He shouldn't exist; he should be killed,' but the idea might have started then, because I hated him so badly at that moment. And before that when he beat me when I was pregnant and was pushing me down the stairs to have a miscarriage and laughed when I wanted to call the police, because they wouldn't interfere in family affairs and, anyway, they would rather believe him, an English solicitor than me, a Polish immigrant . . ."

She shook herself as if trying to get rid of this memory. Again she drained a whole glass of champagne without pausing and said:

"You see, I can't rationally explain what is going on in this head of mine. Sometimes I think that there must be a devil inside me who orders me to kill Robert. So I fight with him against that decision because I still love Robert and want to protect him. Another time I imagine that this voice inside me is the voice of God, or the highest judge, which, after all quite rightly, decided that Robert ought to be punished, but I still try to defend and justify him. For example, by putting the blame on Catherine who harmed him so badly by leaving him for his best friend. I blamed even you, for letting it all happen. I tried to justify Robert in terms of losing trust in people, after being betrayed by both his closest friends and losing the will to behave correctly when he observed that nothing good came out of it. 'When you are good, you are a loser,' he always taught me. I've changed so much since I first met him! I would never have believed that somebody could have so strong influence on you and on your life if it hadn't happened to me."

She handed her empty glass to Paul to be refilled and started again. "I know I can't live like that any longer. I also know that I'm going mad. You can see it yourself. I'm so afraid of myself and also *for* myself. I'm so afraid *of* Robert and also *for* Robert. But mainly I'm afraid of that voice of God or the Devil, which is inside me." And she again drank a whole glass of champagne in three or four deep gulps as if it were water and as if she wanted to quench the fire of that destructive energy which burned inside her.

"It is impossible that God would induce me to kill Robert, isn't it?" she asked and didn't wait for an answer. "But is it also impossible that I could be so strongly influenced by Satan? But the worst is the consciousness that whoever's voice it is, it's getting more and more difficult for me to keep it under control. You know that it would be a tragedy if I let that power dominate me."

Later on, whenever Paul analyzed that meeting with Natalie here, in his office, he was never able to find an answer to what made him suddenly decide, just at that moment when she appeared somehow to have recovered control over that fatalistic voice inside her and probably to try to withdraw from what she had said earlier, to pour oil on to the fire by informing her, just now, about *that bet.*

The most likely explanation was that he wanted to make sure that now, when Natalie had already started to relax after this outburst of hatred for Robert, she would not forget how big a bastard Robert was; Robert, his friend, his idol to imitate for so many years, and at the same time, through all those years, a real bastard.

So he had to tell Natalie that Robert took her to California not because he loved her but only because he wanted to win his bet with Paul! Paul recalled all of his conversation with Robert in this very room, two years before, on the eve of his intended wedding to Natalie.

Paul vividly remembered how, full of Californian sun and confidence, Robert stated (to remind these people who seemed to forget it, as he had said), that he always had to be the winner of his and Paul's "little bets," so now he was going to take Natalie from Paul, as Paul had taken Catherine from him some years before. It was Robert's 'little revenge," he explained, so Paul would remember that he was never allowed to do anything that Robert disliked.

Paul knew that mentioning Catherine would enrage Natalie and also that it would prolong her hatred for Robert, that hatred which, Paul felt, was somehow already diminishing. And it was the main thing Paul had to be concerned about now. He felt it was up to him now to keep Natalie's inner voice saying: "I want to kill him." It was up to him now to keep it going, to stimulate it. Now, when he had already decided that what Natalie had just stated was the only solution!

When Paul was telling Natalie about the bet, her eyes again became wild, expressing all those contradictory feelings, which Paul had seen there before connected with Robert: love and hatred, pain and joy, but above all there was that dominating disbelief and endless surprise, with which she asked:

"Paul, why didn't you tell me about it then?"

"Because I knew then that you wouldn't believe me," he answered sadly and truthfully. "You would have thought that I had invented it all merely to prevent you from leaving me. Of course, if you were to ask Robert about the bet, he would deny everything and you would prefer to believe him, because at that time the only thing you wanted to believe in was that Robert would take you to California." Paul sighed deeply and added, "Also, I somehow believed at that time that everything might work out between you two, and I sincerely hoped it would because I wanted so much for you to be happy."

"Oh, Paul! I didn't expect that you loved me so much." She was close to tears. "Now it will be even harder for me to live, when I realize that I hurt you so much."

"It's fine, darling." Paul decided that the right moment had come: "You see, Natalie, unconsciously throughout all that time when you were with him, I was waiting for this meeting to come. The things you told me today have fully repaid for all those days and nights without you."

"Oh, Paul!"

"I also know," he continued, as if in a frenzy, "that I unconsciously expected those words to come: 'I want to kill him.' Because, you see, I also wanted it to happen. Oh, Natalie, please, don't be so surprised. You are making it more difficult for me. You see, I also hate Robert!" Paul couldn't recognize himself. Never before had he felt so much aggression within himself. "I know I've hated Robert for a long time. Unconsciously I probably always hated him. As long as I have known him. But I've never allowed myself to recognize that feeling. I hated him for what he has done to you and to Tricia and also to all the other women he has had. I knew that he beat Catherine as well and that he psychologically battered all his other women. I also hate him for how he has treated all the people he has known. They existed merely to be exploited, to serve his pleasure. And most of all I hate him because he has had such a strong influence on me and on my life. I also hate myself for being too weak to stand up to him, to tear myself away from his influence."

"From his charm. I know the feeling," Natalie broke in. "He has this psychopathic charm."

"Oh, yes, I know," Paul interrupted forcefully. And again he was surprised that he could be so aggressive. Interrupting a woman! It was not what his mother had taught him. But more important now than good manners was to prevent Natalie from being overwhelmed by this sudden sentimental memory connected with that charm of Robert's. So he had had a good reason for his interruption. "So we've agreed now that we have to liberate ourselves from Robert, haven't we?" He stated as a fact: "It has already been decided, hasn't it?" Another statement in the form of a question, but the sort of question for which the answer has already been determined.

"Yes," she said weakly. Her eyes, huge, staring at Paul, expressed admiration and astonishment (that he could be such a powerful speaker, as he assumed). But those feelings were mingled with fear, still dominating there. And Paul didn't like it. He decided he should challenge her now:

"I suppose you are not going to withdraw now?" And not letting her answer he continued: "We have to liberate not only ourselves. We have to liberate the whole world from him." Paul felt that he was gradually more and more influenced by his own speech. She should be as well he hoped. "Even if it weren't you any longer, his other women will be in the same position. Those people don't change. Even prisons can't reform them."

Paul noticed that Natalie wanted to protest. So he knew that he now had to remind her of Tricia.

"If you leave him, he will ill-treat your daughter even worse than he has done." Yes, it was a good shot. "You remember, in psychology it is common knowledge: replacement of the mother. You told me about it yourself. Besides, you remember, what he did to you. Your whole life has been brought to a halt by him. You can't plan a thing as long as he exists because, as you said, you can't predict your reaction when you see him next. Maybe you are already thinking about giving him another chance?" he asked derisively.

Paul was again surprised with himself. He had never been able to be so biting with anybody, and he had never been able to produce such a long monologue. That's why he wasn't a barrister, even though he had wanted very much to please his mother by becoming one. He suddenly felt that this length of speech was the very maximum he could achieve, and that now he has to conclude as quickly and as briefly as possible, so he took a big breath and said:

"Natalie, you realize that you don't need to do it yourself." It was a half-question. And he had the answer ready: "You can just copy his plan, the way he wanted to kill you." Paul was impressed that it came out so naturally. Again as if somebody else had said it for him. It was only now that he admitted the meaning of those words, long after analyzing their form. It was the form he concentrated on. And only now he realized that he was still talking. Still in the same calm, collected manner. "You remember, you were telling me that Robert liked to frighten you by threatening that he could kill you and nobody even would know that he had anything to do with it because he could ask one of his murderer clients to do it for him?"

"Of course I remember," Natalie answered, again looking terrified.

"I also," Paul continued, "I also know some people who can do it for you. For us," he corrected himself.

# Natalie's Diary 8

## Thursday, 3 December

Why is this departure delayed again? It has never happened before, and I have been to Spain so many times. But suppose it is destiny, suppose that God is giving me a chance to run back to the house and prevent what is going to happen. If I run back now, I would be there before Robert. Before Robert walks in to find the murderer there waiting for him in the sitting room. I should go then. I should run. I should stop it! This plane's delay must be a sign of determinism, and we shouldn't oppose these signs. But, on the other hand, I could interpret the delay as an opportunity for me to write down all his crimes against me and Tricia. To write them down and to think about them once again, to confirm in myself the conviction that I shouldn't even try to contemplate going back to the house and preventing the murder.

Don't I already know that it is right, what is going to happen there? Even God wouldn't forgive the sinner who has sinned so often. Especially as he has never shown any sign of repentance for what he's done and has never treated the fact that he was forgiven as a opportunity to rehabilitate himself (as I naively thought that he would).

God obviously would know that the realization of impunity in some sinners can only lead them to committing even bigger crimes. It was definitely so in Robert's case. One of his earliest crimes always comes back to me any time I cross the entrance to an airport. Like just now, almost so tangible that I can smell the air and sense the mood of that day at Heathrow so many years ago, when Robert and his mother (her presence necessary just to make sure that he would be strong enough not to stop all that procedure, as he had done already once, just before Tricia was born) packed three-week-old Tricia and myself, like two suitcases, on the plane to Poland. I feel sick and close to tears (as I was that day) any time when I'm at an airport. It is probably the best example to show how our past experiences are able to influence the present. I never should have forgiven him for that. Even God wouldn't forgive him for that, since He prescribed some basic rules for guiding the world; eg, even animals care for their babies.

Nobody still seems to know when we can expect our departure. It is supposed to be due to fog. That at least is what the family sitting next to me has just learned. But who knows what the truth is? I don't believe in anything people say any more. Maybe it's better that way . . .

So one of my justifications to myself for this horrible plan is that even God wouldn't pardon Robert for what he has done. Second one could be the explanation that any solicitor would use in my defense if this case come to an American courts. As even Paul said yesterday, that if it would be in America, he could guarantee that I would walk out a free person, after the verdict, as so many American wives have done in the past on the basis of diminished responsibility, having been influenced by the battered wives syndrome. Paul said that in my case it would be used most appropriately, because there is the strong possibility that I would be killed by him (me and the child in my womb) if I didn't kill him first. Didn't he take me to the flat of that paid murderer to warn me that, if I wouldn't agree to an abortion, he had somebody "who is experienced in dealing with disobedient wives"? Because a wife must of course obey her husband, as she promises to do at the altar in an English church, in the verse, which only recently can be omitted by a bride in her wedding vow, if it is discussed and agreed beforehand, giving another example of how England is still behind other European countries, not to mention the USA.

I remember telling Paul that this death threat had already worked on me once, in exactly the same circumstances, so Robert knew it would work again. I never can forget that I actually agreed on an abortion once before, when we were still living in London and he was threatening me that he would kill me if I didn't do it and that nobody even would suspect that it was him, because he was a solicitor so he knew how to do it properly. This was another of his crimes which I should never have forgotten. As I should never forget that he beat and raped me so many times. I think that a woman who has once been beaten or raped will always involuntarily adopt a defensive position at the moment when a man lifts his hand up for any reason, which may be completely disconnected with her past. That is tragic, but it is true, and it is a great pity that we don't have any follow-up studies showing the psychological effect on women, because, I'm sure, the results of those studies would enable some judges to predict, at the moment when a rapist is standing in front of him and defense suggests that the victim had a too-short skirt on so it's her fault, the dramatic influence the rape can have on the girl future.

If s a pity also that in England, incest or sexual abuse within families are still regarded as taboo, so there are not enough talks about it and there aren't any follow-up studies, showing how tragic an effect it can have on a child's life. Isolated drastic examples; like the actress Rita Hayworth's case (who was systematically raped by her father and used to provide him with money and later developed a pattern of marrying similar men to her father and finished as a vegetable cared for by her daughter), are not enough to persuade an English court to believe that it is a likely consequence of incest and sexual abuse within the family . . . I don't even want to think what could have happened to my little Tricia.

Still no sign of our plane, as the man next to me reported after coming back from his periodic expedition to the monitor. If everything was going normally, if we weren't delayed, I would be already over the South of France and I couldn't have a better alibi. But Paul has a good one as well; playing bridge at home, with three other partners who can testify. We shouldn't lose these alibis. We couldn't have planned it better.

But do I have the right to take the law in my own hands, and, more precisely, in the hands of a paid killer? Do I have right to claim that an English judge wouldn't punish Robert adequately? What am I, a God or something, that I claim to know what should be an adequate punishment for rape or assault? But who are they; these English judges, (a God or something) that they are supposed to know what the punishment for rape or assault should be? I can even see some logical explanation why rape isn't condemned more severely in English court. Let's look at it. All legal institutions here are still heavily influenced by men. And men can't propose more severe punishment on rapists because it would be in some way a betrayal of all males, of the very nature of manhood, in which the will of raping is inseparable part.

If the above speculation didn't bear an element of truth, men wouldn't have any reason for insisting that all women like "rough treatment from time to time." I think that there are far fewer women who would agree to the statement that "women like rough treatment," than men who give it as an example of the average woman's personality. The reason is that, if women didn't like rough treatment, men wouldn't have justification for rape in the marital bed. How careful women should be in what they say, because everything can be used against them, like it is in the case of any socially inferior group.

Wouldn't it be better, then, if more women allowed themselves to admit that they liked only gentle lovemaking, so it would create a greater distance between what women really liked and rape and therefore rape would have a stronger chance of recognition as a violation against very nature of womanhood and, in consequence, would get a higher sentence? But unfortunately, nowadays it is fashionable for women to appear more tarty, or more like men, so some of them might even say that they like rough treatment, just because "it is cool" to say it, and a man, picking that up, would answer: "Why not, I don't want to deprive you of what you really like."

Women in England probably don't realize that to change the law, which is heavily biased against them, they have to first change the view of themselves in English society, which is also at that moment still biased against them. The problem is that they have to change themselves first, so the view of themselves will follow suit.

But most of them don't see it. They don't even see that there is anything wrong with them or with the society, since that view of women was with them from the day they were born, so it means "it is the way it should be." But I can't think that it should be that way maybe because I come from a different culture, from the culture where women are put on a pedestal, admired, worshipped with flowers (maybe not so in working classes but certainly in the class I come from, but even in working classes woman is reasonably respected by her husband). Let's take Friday evening, for example; For English woman "Friday evening-lad's evening" idea is not a synonym of ignoring woman but synonymous of marital stability, since most of these women acquired that idea already in their parents house.

But why should I have the right to impose my cultural values on women here? I criticized when the English did the same to their colonies. If somebody is happy with what he believes in, by not knowing the alternative, why not leave him alone? So why did I start all these changes in Robert? Why didn't I let him just be? Be as he was! Maybe he wasn't so bad in the beginning, and if he was, he never knew about it, because all his friends, uncles, and father were the same. Maybe he wasn't bad at all, only I looked at him through my biased eyes, biased by Polish culture? Maybe he was only a little bit worse than other fellows, because he was more than the average man afraid of falling in love? Which shouldn't be a surprise, since when he did fall in love before, he was so badly cheated by his wife and his best friend. So when we first met, he was obviously thinking: "There is another Polish woman, who, like Catherine, wants to marry me for an English passport and later leave with a richer and more handsome fellow." That's why he was fighting with himself for not getting too involved, knowing what is the pain when a woman leaves you.

It was just self-protection. Nobody can deprive him from this right.

So am I again blaming Catherine for all that has happened? She deceived him, he suffered, and it made him so suspicious of women, so afraid of falling in love? Maybe, but it didn't make him beat me and rape me, did it? Yes, it might have. It might make him hate me, for the fact that he couldn't stop loving me, and that he hated himself, because he wasn't strong enough not to get involved. Maybe he wanted to stop it, when it was still possible for him to quit, without being badly hurt? Maybe it's why he wanted me to go to Poland, and at the same time he hated himself for doing it, hated me for being the cause of all his troubles, hated Tricia, as the living proof of the love which he hated so much.

I'd better stop analyzing it, because it will be too late. I'd better go there and, if it is not too late, we maybe can talk openly, for the first time. Maybe we have grown up to the point that we can go together through the events of our life and try to explain, why we acted the way we did. Go! Just go there!

# Chapter 9

## *Bridge Playing*

P aul was angry with himself for this restlessness. Everything was arranged so well that there was no reason for being so anxious. He was repeating to himself again and again that there wasn't even the slightest possibility that anyone would suspect him or Natalie. At this moment, Natalie probably was already over Spain or even landing in Malaga, and Paul had an excellent alibi because all three guests present here can honestly confirm that he hasn't moved from the bridge table for the last three hours.

The fact is that one of the guests was his mother, whose evidence would not carry much weight, because everyone knows that she doted on her son to the extent of lying in court to save him. But the words of two other participants of the bridge evening can never be doubted. They were two prominent and respected figures in the academic and scientific world, fellows at Cambridge University: Dr. Schopenhauser and Professor Peter Brown, the well-known and eminent historian.

So there was no reason at all for his anxiety. Why then this shaking of his hands when he was shuffling the cards? It was already spotted by his mother, as he noticed in her questioning look when they exchanged glances. He hoped only by her. The other pair of bridge players seemed to be deeply absorbed in the game.

And this was when the bell rang, and Paul's hand with a card in it froze over the table. It's the police! They already know, went through his mind. Thank God I don't have to open the door. My legs feel as if they are made from cotton wool. I can't even get up.

Sue, Paul's secretary, was here for the evening, doing her overtime, as cook and the house's hostess. It was the role that she had probably always dreamed of, as Paul's mother remarked to him tonight when Sue blushed in response to Prof Brown's compliment that the role of mistress of the house was very becoming to her.

"A client to see Paul in the study," announced Sue in matter of fact voice.

"At this time?" asked Paul, showing annoyance. "Why did you let him in?"

"The client insisted," answered Sue, putting significant emphasis on the word "client."

So Paul was now certain it must be the police. How could they get him so quickly? he thought. They caught John in the act of killing Robert, and John told them that Paul paid for the job? He still couldn't get up.

"I'll be there after this hand. Thank you, Sue," he said as calmly as he could. "I'm sorry about that," he added to his companions. "It's how I work."

"Yes, we understand," said Prof Brown. "I also have some students coming at night with some brilliant ideas."

"You had better go now," advised Dr. Schopenhauser. "Your client might just have killed someone and needs your help before he is caught."

"It might be the case," admitted Paul, and he felt amused for a moment that Dr. Schopenhauser could be so close to the truth without knowing the facts. It could be John, Paul said to himself, since it's quite possible that, after killing Robert, John suddenly became anxious about some details of his alibi and came to me to get reassurance that everything was O.K. But he wouldn't do it. It would mean he lost his head. Paul was calming himself down. John was told under no circumstances to come here.

"Anyway, we made it," added Dr. Schopenhauser. "We take the last two tricks." And he put his last two cards on the table with a triumphant smile, as if waiting for applause. And he received it from everybody except Paul, who was only able to think now about John and the police.

When he was getting up to go to the study, Sue crossed his path, looking caringly at him. She had been offering some more drinks and sandwiches to Paul's guests. For a moment Paul felt grateful to her for keeping everything going so smoothly, but immediately his mind went back to John, and the police.

But it wasn't John—it was Natalie, shaking all over, hot, sweating and wet from the rain.

"She didn't take a taxi. That's good; nobody's seen her," went through his mind, and he immediately felt guilty about being so self-protective.

"The plane didn't go," she was saying, catching her breath, "so I went there to see Robert, to stop the killing. I love him so much. I never told you how much . . ." Her eyes were huge and black and hot, just like his open fire. Maybe because the open fire reflected in them. Maybe it's why her face was so golden-red like the goddess's mask in the catacomb. He didn't remember which one, but he was frightened then just the same as now.

"I know how you loved him." He deliberately used the past tense. He wanted to cool her down. "I always knew."

"You see, Robert still could change . . ." It was obvious that she wasn't listening. She sat on the floor in front of the fire. Her coat was on, and the water from it was leaving stains on the white carpet. He didn't know what to do with her and with the carpet. "If he only were able to believe that I really love him," she proceeded in monotonous, dreamlike voice. "Not like Catherine. What will I do now?"

"Take your coat off, for a start, and tell me what happened." Again she didn't listen to him.

"What can I do now? What can I do without him?" It came out like a loud, nearly animal, cry. He couldn't take it.

"Stop it! Stop it immediately! You don't want everybody to know about it." And he shook her. He actually took her shoulders and shook her. He couldn't believe he was so angry. "We have to act normally." She heard him this time.

"I can't," she said.

"As much as possible," he replied.

"Give me a drink."

He had whisky there. He wouldn't call Sue to bring the water.

"So what did you see?" he asked quietly, as quietly as he could, pouring the drink. "Was he dead?"

"I don't know! We must go there." She was already up on her feet. And she choked on her drink. "I know. In fact, I know very well. I just don't want to admit it to myself." She said this last sentence in her professional manner. He could guess that it was the way she talked to her clients. "He was lying in the study, blood everywhere, the carpet completely red . . ." Still in her wet coat, she fell down on the floor, the way Robert presumably was lying.

"Cool down, cool down, please! We don't want everybody to come here." He felt that he was getting angry again. "Don't talk about Robert. Just cool down. You're probably exaggerating a lot. Tell me about John. You've seen him, I suppose?" Paul was composing the picture of the crime.

"I saw him running through the garden towards the back fence," she answered as though she were in court.

"He was supposed to walk out through the door." The words came unintentionally out of Paul. And he saw that it made her angry. So he became angry again with his weaknesses or with her knowing them.

"Don't be so obsessively precise about keeping your plan." She was obviously laughing at him. "Don't forget that I walked through the door.

John didn't know who I was, did he?" But she stopped her sarcasm nearly immediately, crying out in her dream-like tone of voice again, "I wanted to prevent this killing. I wanted to walk in and tell John, 'Tton't do it. You still will be paid as arranged.' And I would talk to Robert; I would tell him everything. We maybe would be able to talk now after he realized how far I was pushed. We could start everything again."

He hated her dreams about Robert. "Not again!" he thought. He handed her a drink.

"So you've seen him dead? Did you?" He felt good about his ruthless tone.

She pushed the drink away, spilling some on the shiny surface of the tray.

"I don't want to live without him!" she cried. "I can't."

She was kneeling and bowing rhythmically up and down toward the fire, like a pagan wife in front of the bonfire upon which her husband's body was burning. Paul impressed himself with those two appropriately chosen images in his mind.

"Nati, be quiet, please," he begged. "Be quiet. They will hear you." He didn't know what to do about her. "I'll get you some water," he decided.

"No! Don't!" she stopped him. "Don't go! I can't be on my own," she explained. "No, don't worry, I won't kill myself," she added as the answer to the question which never came. "God wouldn't approve of it."

"He doesn't approve of any killing," said Paul.

She laughed hysterically, chanting, "Not of unborn children, not of cruel husbands, not even of stupid wives. My God, how will you judge me? You know I was right."

Paul didn't know if it were a statement or a question, if it were for him or for God. But he knew he had to stop it. She really was in a bad state. And with those people in the other room.

"Nobody's seen you, I suppose?" he asked coldly.

She didn't seem to hear him; she was still in that study with Robert.

"You should see the smile on his face," she said. "The frozen smile! His devious frozen smile." She was laughing now, cynically. Surely, she must hate him! "His smile was saying; 'I'm happy to give you some problems, baby.' That's what his smile was saying. I ran away! His laughter was running after me. I couldn't do anything else. I imagined his running after me, dripping blood all over the white pebbled path to the house. I don't think anybody's seen me, if that's what you are concerned about." Her tone amazed him. The answer was perfectly controlled, light, as if she were talking about promenading on a sunny Sunday afternoon, not about today's black, wet night of horror.

"You know, you must go away." Paul started by establishing some facts. "In your position, I wouldn't let an English judge deal with the case. You know their prejudice against women."

"Don't start your cool, civilized advice now, Paul," she interrupted. "Not now, when we should go to Robert. We might still save him." She looked so confused.

"Nati, you know we can't. You know he is dead, you know that."

"No, I don't!" she protested loudly. "I don't know anything."

"I do," stated Paul. "I know that John is a perfectionist. Robert told me that long ago. He is very proficient in his job. I know that. You have to face the facts . . ."

"No! No!" she shouted. "We have to go there. I have to see him once more! I have to see him."

"Don't shout, please. Don't shout, Nati. You know, I'm your best friend. Listen to me. You have to do what I'm saying—you have to go back to the airport!" He stressed each word the way he saw hypnotists do it. For a moment he felt that he wouldn't mind being one. "Your plane must still be there, unless they've redirected it to Seville, which they do sometimes when there is thick fog." . . . But he discarded this thought immediately. "Your plane should still be there. If not, take the next one, but remember: you've never been here! Remember that! You just went for a walk in the rain. You told me that you like walking in the rain before going abroad. To think about England. It's perfect. You went for a walk in the rain, to think about wet England. Remember, you've never been here. Or in the house. Remember that! You have to go now. I can't go with you. You understand that? Take a cab somewhere close to the airport. After, take another one to the airport. Take his number, and make sure he will remember you. Talk to him about Spain and fog and your walk in the rain. I can't go with you. You understand that?"

"Yes, I do understand, Paul," she answered in a polite schoolgirl tone, somewhat lethargically and very sad. He didn't want to see that. He mustn't think about it. So he continued.

"If the plane is gone, take the next one to anywhere. Maybe to Poland. You always have your Polish passport with you."

"No, I can't go there," she interrupted him, protesting, fully awakened. "Not there, not with my guilt. In fact, I can't go anywhere.

I need to face it."

Paul was shocked.

"Don't face it in England. I told you! Not in an English court!"

"Judges are changing, even in England. We all are changing. A judge should be like God. He will understand. And I'm pregnant now, with Robert's child. The best news is that he can't stop me from having it now." She laughed cynically, and she cried at the same time, "Unless he makes me kill myself."

She looked so mixed up that Paul now had to admit he really had no idea how to cope with her.

And that was when his mother came into it, like so many times before, to save him. Just when he needed her the most, she just walked into the room. And he instantly experienced that sweet tiredness and relaxation like so many times before when she suddenly appeared to help him. He still wouldn't have believed it if somebody told him that it would happen again. But it did! She was here, and, with her around, everything suddenly was simple, easy and believable. No unusual coincidences at all. Even the fact that she happened to know Natalie from some long time ago seemed quite natural to Paul that night. He remembered this immediate, strong rapport between the two women and that he knew that he could relax now and even finish playing bridge, as his mother had asked him to do.

"You go, son, and finish playing bridge. They're waiting there. Sue can be your partner now; I'll stay here. We have a lot to talk about. You just go! You don't need to worry," she reassured him again, decisively pushing him out of the room.

What he mostly remembered from this last conversation with Natalie after his mother entered the room was that immediate recognition and rapport.

"It was you on that plane from Frankfurt? So many years, but I've never forgotten your eyes. I told you then, they were the eyes of somebody who had touched death."

"And I told you then," Natalie responded instantly, as if to a best friend, "that I had touched death every day. I lived under the constant threat of it."

"I remember," his mother interrupted. "I remember that. Your husband threatened you day and night. You didn't know, I wanted to help you so much that I took the trouble to put a message for you on the radio: to the unknown, beautiful Polish girl on the Frankfurt plane. But you never contacted me."

"You did? You sent a message especially for me?" She looked so surprised. "It could have changed a lot, if you knew how I needed a friend in those days."

"I knew that," his mother interrupted again, "and I see you need a good friend just now. You wouldn't be in a solicitor's office at this time of night if you didn't."

"Mother, I'm her friend, not her solicitor." Paul tried to explain, but his mother cut him off sharply.

"She doesn't need male friends now." She turned to Natalie again. "What's your name, dear? I even don't know your name. Isn't it funny?" She laughed, looking amazed. "I overheard your conversation with Paul," she started again. "You are pregnant, darling? And confused?"

"Yes," admitted Natalie, probably for both questions.

"I know. You were confused then. I'll never forget your description of the view out of the plane's window; you said the fields down below were like pieces of a jigsaw puzzle that you used to like to put together as a young girl back in Poland. You said they always matched so easily, like your life and yourself in those days. And after your coming to England, your jigsaw never matched again. Isn't it a beautiful description? Don't you think, Paul? Oh, Paul," she shouted suddenly, as if stricken by some realization, "You should be there! They are waiting. "You should be playing bridge! Go on, son, go!" And she pushed him out of the room so quickly that he hardly had time to say good-bye to Natalie.